ESCAPE F

ESCAPE
FROM LOCH LEVEN

Mollie Hunter

CANONGATE · KELPIES

First published 1981 by
Hamish Hamilton Children's Books
under the title *You Never Knew Her As I Did*
First published in Kelpies 1987

Copyright © Maureen Mollie Hunter McIlwraith 1981
Cover: detail from 'Mary aged 16' by Francois Clouet,
reproduced by kind permission of the Bibliotheque
Nationale, Paris.
Cover border: Jill Downie

Printed in Great Britain
by Cox & Wyman Ltd, Reading, Berkshire

ISBN 0 86241 137 8

*The publisher acknowledges subsidy
of the Scottish Arts Council
towards the publication of this volume.*

CANONGATE PUBLISHING LIMITED
17 JEFFREY STREET, EDINBURGH EH1 1DR

Foreword

This book tells of an episode in the life of Mary, Queen of Scots; and since she is one of the most controversial characters in all history, readers may wonder how much of the story is fact and how much is invention.

The answer here is that I have spent many years researching both the episode and its historical background, and in creating my novel I have kept faithfully to the findings of my research. Where there is any gap in the records of the period, the bridging inference I have drawn has invariably been the one I conceived as that most in line with known events and most true to the characters of those involved.

M.H.

To my nephew and godson, Connal McIlwraith, a book of his own at last! With love from Mollie Hunter.

THE STEWART LINE

ROBERT I (The Bruce)

Marjory, married to Walter the High Steward

ROBERT II

Robert, Duke of Albany

ROBERT III

David, Duke of Rothesay

JAMES I

JAMES II

JAMES III

JAMES IV
married Margaret Tudor, daughter of Henry VII

James V

MARY, QUEEN OF SCOTS

JAMES VI

THE DOUGLAS TABLE

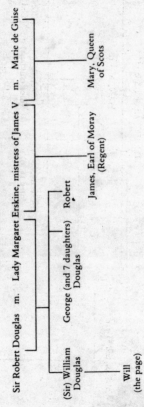

Sir Robert Douglas   m.   Lady Margaret Erskine, mistress of James V   m.   Marie de Guise

(Sir) William Douglas

George (and 7 daughters) Douglas

Robert

James, Earl of Moray (Regent)

Mary, Queen of Scots

Will (the page)

HOW THE CROWNS OF SCOTLAND AND ENGLAND WERE UNITED

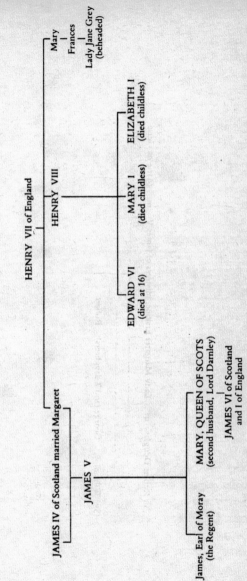

1

News of her has come at last from England; and it is the worst I ever dreaded to hear. She has been executed – her head chopped off with an axe. " . . . *of the kind woodsmen use. . . .*" the report says.

A voice far back in my mind is screaming denial of that report; and yet still I know it is true. I can trust the agent who wrote it. And the courier who brought it – the young fellow facing me now – was trained by me, personally. I know that he, too, is reliable. Besides, I have the proof of it all in the letters he also brought me. I must face it squarely, it seems. Mary, Queen of Scots – *my* Queen – is dead.

I wish the courier would stop staring at me – but perhaps he has never seen a man weep before this. He is so young – a boy, just turned sixteen. A boy can go safely where a man would be suspected. That was why I chose him for training, as I have chosen all my couriers for almost twenty years past now – oh God, twenty years! Has it been that long, the time she spent captive in England?

And for me? A full twenty years in her service, with nineteen of these spent scheming on her behalf in every royal court in Europe; even this raw young fellow knows it has been like that for me, does he not? And so he stares. Or does he wonder if I weep because I too may be one of the many who loved her simply as a man loves a woman?

"She is dead." I say the words aloud, suddenly not caring at all what he thinks of my choking voice. The years of service are at an end now. There is nothing more I can do for her. But that is hard to accept; so very hard. I wonder... Is that why my memory is flooding now with the brave days past when all her fortunes rested on what *I could* do for her? Is it the helpless feeling I have now that makes me want so much to recall those days? The courier's presence is an intrusion on that desire.

"Go through to Minny," I tell him. "She will take care of your needs."

He looks blankly at me until I recollect he knows Minny only by the courtesy title I have given her. "Mistress Douglas," I say impatiently; and he turns to leave me.

The tide of memory begins to surge again; and now, thank God, I have the relief of letting myself drift with it...

2

The 17th day of June in the year of 1567; that was when they brought her, captive, to our island Castle of Lochleven. I recall that very precisely.

We were waiting for her in a tight and silent group on the landing-stage there – Sir William Douglas, his brothers Robert and George, and myself Will Douglas, page to Sir William – and also his bastard son, of course, although that relationship was never openly admitted.

At our backs, we had the grim and ancient walls of the Castle. Facing us across the narrow strip of water between island and mainland was the New House – the mansion Sir William had built to accommodate his mother and seven sisters as well as his own growing brood of children. It was five o'clock in the morning; dawn, with nothing moving except the boat scudding out from the mainland towards us. The eyes of the Douglas brothers were steady on the boat. Mine roved between it and their faces. How would they take the Queen's arrival here?

Sir William had honestly approved of the rebellion the Scottish lords had raised against her. More than that, he was hereditary Keeper of Lochleven Castle, and conscientious in his duties. Sir William, I thought, would have little trouble now in viewing the Queen as a Prisoner of State. And I could discount Robert Douglas. He was not part of the Castle garrison. Robert was there that morning only to act as witness to her actual landing. But what about George?

George was Commander of the Castle Guard. But George was still only twenty-four – the same age as the Queen; *and* handsome enough to have "Pretty Geordie" for his nickname. He was chivalrous too; a true romantic. And so how did *he* view the prospect of acting as jailer to a Queen who was also the most beautiful woman in Europe?

The boat came near enough to identify the two armoured men keeping guard over the Queen. George turned to his brothers. "The two we expected," he said. "Lord Ruthven, and our own dear brother-in-law Lord Lindsay."

"A cunning man, Ruthven," Robert Douglas remarked. "Watch out for him, William."

"While you depart from here," Sir William grumbled, "washing your hands of the trouble I might have."

"Lindsay will be the one to give trouble," George said. "There is no-one half so ruthless as he is."

The other two nodded agreement to this; and, plaintively, Sir William added, "God knows why sister Euphemia chose to marry *that* man."

"*God knows indeed,*" I thought. Everyone was afraid of Lindsay – even his own young daughter, Margaret. Or so I had been told, at least, by Sir William's daughter, Ellen. And how could I doubt Ellen when I knew the close friendship there was between her and Lindsay's girl?

Suddenly, I found, I was sorry for the Queen; and the feeling surprised me. I had never been given to spending sympathy on anyone except myself, after all, and this Mary Queen of Scots was no part of my troubles. But even so . . . She had been kind to me, in the past. How was she bearing up now, I wondered, under the fact of being so completely at the mercy of men like Ruthven and Lindsay?

I had my answer to that within seconds of the boat touching at the landing-stage.

Ruthven was first ashore, the warrant for the Queen's committal outstretched in his hand. Lindsay was close on Ruthven's heels. The two young waiting-ladies seated behind the Queen gathered up small pieces of baggage, while the Queen herself rose to step on to the landing-stage. Her long, amber-coloured eyes flashed an upward glance at Ruthven and Lindsay. Her voice came with a cutting edge to its natural sweetness.

"I will have your heads for this!"

In a flare of black satin skirts and stockings of gold thread, she was ashore then unaided, in a leap as nimble as any I have ever seen. Scornfully she looked down at the two waiting lords – as indeed from her slender height she could look down on most men. Ruthven's pale face had gone corpse-white. Lindsay was dusky red with anger. He choked, on venom struggling for voice, and got the words of his retort out at last.

"You adulterous bitch, you! You French whore!"

She turned her back on him. The rabble soldiery had yelled the same words at her, only thirty-six hours before, when she had been forced to surrender to Lindsay himself and the others of her rebel lords. But this time she did not weep or tear her hair, as she had so despairingly done then. Calmly, instead, as Lindsay went on raving at her back, she faced Sir William and told him,

"I have been brought here by force, Sir William, and you know that. You know also that you have no right to detain me."

"Your Grace, I have the instructions of the Privy Council." Sir William was red with embarrassment over Lindsay's scene as he struggled to state his case to her. "And if they are agreed you are to be held in Lochleven Castle, I have no choice but to do my duty as its Keeper."

"Your first duty," she retorted, "is to me. And I defy the warrant of your instructions. The Privy Council – as you very well know – is ruled now by those same lords who are in rebellion against me."

"Because of your misgovernment, your Popish idolatry, your whoring with the Earl Bothwell!" Behind her back, Lindsay was still obscenely shouting, and now there were tears in her eyes. But now also, I realised, she had found one man there to champion her.

Another voice roared out suddenly, the voice of young George Douglas. In a parade-ground bellow that easily drowned the sound of Lindsay's snarl, he began a series of orders to the contingent of the Castle Guard lined up behind the landing-stage. The stamp of feet, the clashing of arms, were added to the din of George's commands. And then, in the small silence that followed the end of this noisy display, the Queen made a move that abruptly snatched the initiative from us all.

She began walking alone towards the gate of the Castle. And short though the distance was between that gate and the landing-stage, her action still stated her case better than any words could have done. Lochleven, it reminded everyone there, was a Royal Castle. She, and she alone, was its owner. And every step she took now was both a denial of anyone's right to escort her there like a criminal, and an assertion of her own right to enter it at any time she pleased.

We stood like figures in a tableau watching her; the soldiers frozen in the last position George had given them, her own ladies fixed in the very postures they had taken on stepping ashore. I would have raised a cheer for her then, if I had not been as dumbstruck with surprise as all the others! And yet, with every second I watched her, I was aware also of another feeling creeping in on me.

She was walking, as always, with a willowy grace to all her movements, light and sure on her feet as a dancer. Yet even as I observed this, it seemed to me I could see her as she had been on the last occasion she had entered Lochleven.

Two years before that time, it had been, on one of her many justice-tours around the country. And she had been dressed all in her favourite white with rubies and pearls thick-clustered on the satin gleam of her gown, a hawk on her wrist with jewelled jesses trailing from its legs. All around her too, as she moved with that dancer's step to the gate, there had been a chattering, shifting, laughing throng of court- iers competing for her favour.

All around her . . . That was the key, I thought, to the feeling her gesture had stirred in me. It was not the difference in dress that mattered; not the contrast between her former splendour and the present plain- ness of her appearance. It was that sense of her utter aloneness; that oddly poignant sense . . .

George Douglas had something of the same

feeling. I thought so, at least, from the way that *he* stared after her, and was more than ever certain that gallantry had been his motive for drowning out Lindsay's voice with the sound of his own. George, I concluded, was not taking at all kindly to his own share of putting her under lock and key!

Captain Drysdale of the Castle Guard was the one who broke the spell she seemed to have cast over us all. In a harsh voice that startled the silence, he ordered the soldiers to double forward. The wooden ranks broke, and became soldiers clumsily trotting in pursuit of the Queen. Their moving forms began to hide her from my view. Like a small beacon vanishing in mist, the moments of her aloneness vanished into the general stream of time. But still the impact of her action had not been lost. As I turned again to the group on the landing-stage, Sir William was speaking to Lord Ruthven; and his voice was sharp with protest.

"I know all that, my lord. I do not need it read to me like a lesson that we rebelled because we could not – would not – accept the Earl of Bothwell as the Queen's husband. But Bothwell has now been routed in battle. And she *is* still the Queen – which means she still has powerful friends here at home, as well as among her kinsmen in France. And so, how long *can* I keep her against her will?"

"Put it like this," Ruthven suggested. "We have popular feeling on our side so far as her marriage to Bothwell is concerned, and she herself sees now what a mistake it was. She must stay here until she agrees to divorce him."

"She'll not do that!" Sir William retorted. "Not now she has let it be known she is already seven weeks gone with Bothwell's child. If she divorces him now, it could be declared a bastard. And she'll not take *that* risk."

"You look too far ahead," Ruthven said smoothly. "There is no certainty she will carry the child to term. But even if she does –" He glanced around, smiling slightly; and then, with a movement of his hands that clearly showed his meaning, he added, "A pillow over its face, and a little downward pressure –"

"You will not make *me* party to killing a child!" Indignantly, Sir William interrupted. George Douglas chimed in on exactly the same note, only to be silenced by Lindsay shouting,

"Enough! We did not come here to argue!" Scowling, he turned then to Robert Douglas. "You, sir, were required only to witness the delivery of our warrant. Also, the fact of the Queen entering her prison. And your one final duty, therefore, is to make quick report to the lords with a statement of your witness."

"William?" Robert Douglas looked at Sir William, as if seeking his consent to leave; and was told irritably,

"Yes, yes. You have done all we asked of you."

"In that case..." Robert backed away from the group on the landing-stage, then turned towards the waiting boatman. I guessed from his face before he hurried into the boat, how relieved he was to have finished with his share in the proceedings, and did not blame him for that, considering how ugly they had been till then.

The silence following his departure lasted until the boat was well away from the landing-stage; and then, abruptly, Lindsay told Sir William,

"Now we can talk privately as those who *do* have

9

responsibility for this matter. And so we will have plainer speech than Lord Ruthven gave you."

"My lord – " Ruthven began warningly, but Lindsay brushed his words aside.

"The lords in Privy Council," he went on, "have debated further on the Queen since you were instructed to be her Keeper; and the result of their debate is that they are agreed she has shown herself quite unfit to rule this country. Their first intention, therefore – that of forcing her to separate herself from Bothwell – is now being published only as a blind to their final aim; which is this: she must give up the Throne entirely."

"My lord," Ruthven tried again to interrupt, "you were not authorised to tell Sir William – "

"My God, Ruthven!" Fiercely Lindsay rounded on the other man. "D'ye think that I – a man of the Reformed Faith – will tolerate that Catholic whore defiling my country's throne a day longer than I can help? I have God's authority for speaking out now, I tell you – never mind the fact of common-sense dictating that her jailers *must* know the truth of her situation now!"

Sir William and George were glancing most uneasily at one another while all this was going on. And long before the interchange was finished, I had discreetly interposed Sir William's bulk between Ruthven and myself. If the man objected so much to the others knowing the real facts, I reasoned, *my* presence there might suddenly become unwelcome to him. And I did not want to be disappointed of any further revelations!

Sir William coughed to bring attention back to himself, and then prompted, "You were about to say, Lindsay . . .?"

Ruthven made a show of turning away as if he had shrugged off all further responsibility; and, still flushed with rage, Lindsay faced again to Sir William.

"I was about to say," he snapped, "that Mary Stuart must promise to abdicate the Throne in favour of the infant son of her earlier marriage. And that we – Ruthven and myself – have been instructed to stay here until we get her signature on a Deed which will confirm that promise."

Once again, George and Sir William exchanged glances; then, slowly, Sir William asked, "And suppose you succeed in that, who will be appointed Regent to rule on the child's behalf?"

Lindsay began to grin, a grin that grew into a leer as he told Sir William, "You *know* the answer to that!"

We all did. It was the Earl of Moray who would certainly be appointed Regent; Moray, the Queen's elder half-brother. But Moray was also the elder half-brother of Sir William, and of George. Moray was the bastard borne by their mother, Lady Margaret Douglas, to the Queen's father. And the full story of that long-ago affair was there now, in the leering grin on Lindsay's face.

"And so," he was continuing, "there is no need for me to tell you how very much to the interest of the whole Douglas family it will be, if she does abdicate. Or how very important it is for you to keep her secure until we have her signed promise on that."

"And then?" George asked suddenly. "Will she be set free then?"

"Oh, for heaven's sake, George!" Lindsay exclaimed scornfully. "She is no harmless cage-bird to be loosed out of mere pity! Let her away from here at any time, and she will immediately gather a counter-force to the rebellion – if *that* is what you want!"

A flush leapt into George's handsome face. "I only asked," he said angrily, "in order to know what choice is open to her."

"What choice?" Lindsay echoed; and smiled his leering smile again. "That is easily answered too, my lad. She can abdicate and be imprisoned for life. Or she can die."

3

I heard nothing further then of the Queen's affairs. Lindsay strode off towards the Castle gate as soon as he had spoken. The others followed him – but not before Sir William had ordered me to fetch his mother from the New House. I unmoored one of our boats with my mind very much alive to all I had heard, and the effect it could have on my own situation in the Castle; and all the while I was rowing across to the New House, I went on thinking of this.

I was already sixteen years old, after all, and yet my bastard birth had given me no hope of fortune. What was more, I had a passion for gambling, and I had just lost every penny I once owned. I had also begun to find an insufferable dullness in the only life offered by a small castle tucked away on an island of two acres set in a loch that was itself deep in the heart of the Scottish countryside – all of which had brought me very near the point of deciding I would leave the island altogether for some more lively place. London, perhaps? My only talent – apart from skill at cards – was for playacting, and I had heard there was a lot of that going on these days, in London.

Yet here now, right under my nose, as it were, was a situation that would put Lochleven at the very centre of events. And so why go seeking abroad for the kind of excitement I was now more likely to find at home? The Castle could be assaulted in some attempt to rescue the Queen. Or she might make her own bid for freedom – and it was I who had charge of the Castle boats!

I had a certain advantage, also, in being the bastard of the house. I was not quite a gentleman, yet the family accepted me among them. I was not merely a servant, yet I still had some of a servant's duties, I was therefore free of both sides of the household; and that, in the game of intrigue that was bound to be played now, could make an important figure of me!

I moored the boat at the landing-stage for the New House, ran past the stables behind the house itself, and sent a servant to rouse Lady Margaret Douglas. But the Old Lady – as we all called her – was already awake. And as I should have known, of course, she was expecting my summons. Sir William never moved a step without *her* advice; which meant, I thought wryly, that we would probably have to resign ourselves now to her almost constant presence in the Castle!

It took her only minutes to get the whole story of the Queen's arrival out of me; and when she stepped into my boat for the return journey, she was fairly crowing her satisfaction at the prospect of Moray becoming Regent.

"But *you* are not to speak of that yet," she reminded me sharply; "or you can expect no more favours from me, my lad."

I gave her my promise of silence and in a moment or two she was adding resentfully, "Although

14

Moray should have been King, of course. And might have been too, if that young woman had never been born."

I said nothing to this. It was the Old Lady's favourite grievance that Queen Mary's birth had robbed her precious Moray of the Throne. And her favourite delusion too, of course; but it was not my place to remind the Old Lady that the law did not permit a bastard to be King.

"Remember," she warned after we had landed and I was escorting her to the Great Hall of the Castle, "no gossip from you in the servants' quarters, my lad, or I will have Sir William whip you. But if you are good – " She fumbled inside her cloak and brought her bony hand out again with a gleam of silver in it. "Here!" She thrust the hand at me. "Here is some gambling money."

"*As if she could buy my loyalty!*" But that, of course, was the other side of my situation in the Castle. Simply because I had a foot in both camps, as it were, I was trusted by neither. I almost pushed the bribe back at her, but had not the heart to do so. She was smiling – the old besom! – and I knew how fond she was of me. I thanked her instead, as prettily as she expected, and then did what I had been itching for the past half-hour to do.

I ran to tell Minny of my plans – Minny the laundry maid, the one person in the Castle who did trust me; Minny, who had got that pet name for "mother" long ago from me, because it was she who had clucked over and cared for me as a child. And Ellen Douglas too, of course. And Margaret Lindsay. Minny had so long been "Minny" to all three of us that no-one ever called her anything else now.

But I was still her favourite, I knew; and there had been times, indeed, when I wondered if she actually *was* my mother. My build, after all, was slight – just like hers. Like her, too, I was dark-haired, dark-eyed, quick in all my movements. The Douglases, on the other hand, were all big and fair – like Ellen Douglas, who was as tall as I was although she was still only fourteen.

"– *like Ellen Douglas*..." I checked in the doorway of Minny's laundry, the words repeating in my head and disappointment rising in me at the sight of Ellen there with her. I had been so set on speaking immediately and in private to Minny about my plans! She and Ellen both turned towards me. Minny paused from her task of counting pillow covers into Ellen's arms, and threw a mock-challenge at me.

"So! I hear you have lost all your money again. But there is no use coming to me for more, my lad. *I* have nothing to spare for gambling."

I spanned her waist with my hands and swung her up – she was only a featherweight – to sit on her own ironing-board. She looked comical, perched there with her feet dangling, and I laughed at her,

"Minny, Minny, Minny! Money, money, money! Is that all you can think of to say?"

She swung out her hand to give me a dunt on the ear, missed her mark, and then began scrambling down from the board the way a little girl scrambles down from too high a seat. Ellen and I laughed heartily at this, and Minny herself was grinning. I steadied her last step, and told her,

"No, sweet heart, I am not looking for a gambling-stake. Not yet, anyway. I came to give you news – to tell you that the Queen is here."

Minny nodded towards Ellen. "Your news is late.

Ellen has just this moment told it to me."

"But the Queen," Ellen said primly, "is not here *as* the Queen. She is a Prisoner of State now; and that is how we have to look on her."

I was fond of Ellen, as a rule; and not just because she was my half-sister. She was lively, which had made for good games between us as children. Also, I liked to look at pretty girls, and Ellen had the kind of peach-blossom complexion and blonde curls that made her very pretty. But I did not care for Ellen when she pattered the pious opinions of others; and behind her fair face now I thought I could see the plain, sallow one of Lord Lindsay's daughter, Margaret. Rudely I demanded,

"Who told you then, Mistress Prim, what we must do or not do? Your little friend, Margaret?"

Ellen went red with annoyance. "Margaret Lindsay," she retorted, "is *not* little. She is a year older than me, and you know that! And Margaret has heard her father talking. He says the Queen has brought all her troubles on herself, and – "

"I know what Lord Lindsay says!" Sharply I interrupted Ellen. "I heard all his ravings at the Queen when she landed."

"Well?" Ellen challenged. "He was telling the truth, was he not? She *has* been very wicked, and – and wanton, too."

Minny laughed at this, and teased, "Now Ellen, what can you know of words like 'wanton'?"

Ellen looked even more annoyed then. "I know as much as anyone else," she retorted. "I know why the Queen had Lord Darnley for a husband before she married Bothwell – because Darnley was tall and handsome, and – "

"And because she fell in love with him," Minny

interrupted. "Is that so bad, Ellen? And just think what she got for her pains there!"

Ellen shrugged and looked away. I said loudly, "A poxy rogue of a man!" But Minny hushed me sternly for this, and herself went on telling Ellen the extent of the disaster that love had brought to the Queen. Darnley, she reminded, had been proved a vicious fool, a corrupt creature unworthy of any woman. Everybody had hated Darnley. And so it was small wonder that the Queen – even before her child by him was born – had also come to hate him.

"It was no marriage at all then," Minny pointed out, "and in the end – "

"In the end," Ellen chimed in, "Darnley was murdered. By Bothwell. Everybody says it was Bothwell who murdered Darnley. And everybody says, too, that Bothwell was the Queen's lover *before* she took him for a husband. So what does that make of her, Minny!"

"You be quiet, Will," Minny commanded before I could get out the furious shout that rose in me with this. Then she turned to Ellen. "I am ashamed," she said coldly, "to hear you repeat such stories. You should have your mouth washed out for talking slander like that."

"How do *you* know it is slander?" Ellen demanded; and, sharply, Minny countered,

"I know it because nothing has ever been proved against the Queen. Nor has she ever had a chance to clear her name of the things charged to it. And to speak ill of anyone without proof *is* slander."

"And I told you, did I not, where she gets it?" I pushed Minny aside with this, determined now to add my share. "She listens to Margaret Lindsay parrotting what her father says. And Lord Lindsay hates

18

the Queen. If she was a saint he would find something bad to say about her. As for Margaret Lindsay,
she just tattle-tales out of jealousy, because she is
plain and the Queen is beautiful.''

"That is not true," Ellen retorted. "Margaret does
not like to hear unkind things of anyone.''

"She would be wise then," Minny remarked, "to
keep her own mouth shut. And you had better learn
that too, my girl, if you want to live a peaceful life.''

Ellen's face changed suddenly with this. All the
liveliness went out of it. Her mouth drooped at the
corners. Her brows drew together in a frown. "Who
wants a peaceful life?" she asked sullenly. She looked
from Minny to me. "I could die sometimes, it is so
dull here," she added. "You feel that too, do you not,
Will?''

I nodded, finding I was beginning to forgive her,
after all. Poor Ellen, having to divert herself with
gossip, the same way as I had to find diversion with
secret trips over to the Inn at the mainland village of
Kinross!

"Pax, then?" I offered; and eagerly Ellen agreed,
"Yes, pax, Will. I – I do not believe those stories
any more than you do. And I am sorry now I spoke
harm of the Queen, because she was always kind to
us – was she not? Both of us.''

Memory came crowding back, the way it had
done at the landing-stage. I said, "She used to let you
fairly cram yourself with gingerbread!" The smile
spreading over Ellen's face then persuaded me to
make up with her in style. I took out the Old Lady's
silver coin. "And you can have this now," I told her.
"It was to have been my gambling stake, but you can
use it instead, to buy gingerbread for yourself and
Margaret.''

19

Ellen caught the coin as I flipped it to her, and I grinned to see in her face the thought of John Kemp's bakehouse in Kinross. Ellen always drooled at the mere smell of hot gingerbread! Minny watched indulgently as she thanked me, and told us,

"Now that's more like my two good bairns! And who knows. Having the Queen here could be just what is needed to liven things up for both of you."

Ellen's eyes gleamed afresh at this. "Yes," she said eagerly, "it could be exciting – for all of us!" She looked at me, waiting for my agreement on this, and for a moment I was tempted to take her, also, into my confidence. But some inner voice of caution told me otherwise. If the Queen did abdicate, the voice warned, and if Moray did become Regent, there would be soaring fortunes for the whole Douglas family – Ellen included. It would be foolish, therefore, to let her know that *my* share of the excitement would be found in helping the Queen to escape!

"No doubt at all of it," I said airily; and with a smile of delight at this, Ellen went off with her pillow covers, loudly protesting as she went that she would never quarrel with me again.

"Though I have heard *that* story before," Minny said, laughing as she closed the door on all this. "But now that you have finished with that particular squabble – " She turned to me, her eyes inviting. " – you can tell me, can you not, just why you came rushing in the way you did?"

"Indeed I can!" I was suddenly full of my plans again, and rattling them off to her as quickly as I could. "And so," I finished, "you can see now what *I* was thinking when Ellen said it could be exciting here for all of us."

"I can see why you did not tell her what you have just told me," Minny said drily. "And I am warning you, Will. You may think the Old Lady is ambitious for the Earl of Moray, but I have lived long enough among the Douglas family to know he is even more ambitious for himself. I should be sorry for *anyone* he finds standing between himself and the prospect of being Regent."

It was not like Minny to be so serious with me. Minny had always been more inclined to laugh than to scold at any of my various escapades. "You are seeing me underground before I am even dead," I teased her. "But I have a lot of living to do yet, Minny. And that still includes some gambling!"

"But you have just given Ellen – " she began, and stopped herself to stare at me drawing my knife and then slicing off one of the silver buttons on my doublet.

"My next gambling-stake – see!" I held the button up between thumb and forefinger, broadly grinning at her.

"But that set of buttons," she protested, "was the Old Lady's present to you on your last birthday. She will kill you for that!"

I shook my head. "What the eye does not see, the heart does not grieve for. And the Old Lady will not see me lacking one of my buttons because you, sweet heart, can easily find an exact copy to take its place."

Minny's eyes slid to the box where she kept all her replacement buttons. "I could, I suppose," she sighed; and within minutes of that, she had stitched on a button that was enough like the others to deceive even the sharp eyes of the Old Lady. I gave her a hearty kiss of thanks for her work, and she was

21

still laughing at what she called my "impudence" when I ran off to find out whatever I could about the Queen's new circumstances.

4

She had been locked up with her two young *femmes de chambre* in the small round tower built into the south-eastern angle of the wall that circled all the Castle buildings. But that would at least give her privacy, since the small tower lay the whole width of the courtyard away from the square tower that was both our main defence structure and the family living quarters.

As for Ruthven and Lindsay, I was glad to learn from George, we would not have them all the time with us in the main tower. Lindsay had decided to stay with his wife in the New House, and Ruthven had also made the New House his preference.

"Comfort first for both of them, you see, although they are both so intent on making misery for the Queen," George added sourly. And sourness being so unusual in George, I felt I had been right in thinking that here was one Douglas at least, whose sympathies would be with her. In everything else I had expected, however, I turned out to be completely wrong.

There were no great raids, no dramatic bids for escape, no excitement at all, in fact; or none, at least, of the kind I had hoped for. Sir William's shocked face, as he hurried back next morning from his first official visit to the round tower, gave notice of what we had to expect instead. The Queen had fallen ill. Breathlessly, he gave out the news. So violently ill, that it seemed she would die!

We were a full company in Lochleven that morning. The Old Lady and Margaret Lindsay had come across with the lords Ruthven and Lindsay from the New House. The table for breakfast in the Great Hall was still littered with the remains of bread and ale. There was silence while Sir William leaned on the table, as if for support. I rushed to help him into his chair; and then, smoothly into the silence, came Lord Ruthven's voice.

"In that case, Sir William, we shall all be saved a lot of trouble. Shall we not?"

"Well spoken, Ruthven!" Lindsay exclaimed. "Oh, well spoken!" He gave a great guffaw of laughter on the words, and I was not surprised to see Margaret Lindsay wince at all this. She had always been a nervous sort of girl; and she shrank even more then, when George banged the table and shouted angrily,

"Are you Christians, you two, or are you wolves!"

"*Geordie*!" Eyes brilliantly glaring in the ruined beauty of her face, the Old Lady commanded George to silence. Then, briskly as usual, the mixture of cunning and kindliness that was *her* nature took charge of the situation.

"William," she instructed, "you will send immediately to Edinburgh for the Queen's own physician. And her own cook."

"But hold hard!" Lindsay interrupted. "If the Queen does recover, that means there will still be the

Deed of Abdication standing, unsigned, between Moray and the Regency. Between *your son* and the Regency!"

"Y'are a fool, Lindsay," the Old Lady retorted. "You always were a fool."

"Eh?" Lindsay stared at her, mouth hanging open, rage beginning to take over from his astonishment; but still there was no weakening of the Old Lady's brilliant glare. Acidly she told Lindsay,

"I have more sons than Moray. And if the Queen dies so soon after entering William's custody, it is *he* who will be blamed. Poison – that is what will be suspected. And taking the Queen prisoner is one thing – no more, in fact, than the fortunes of war. But poisoning her is another matter altogether; one that would be certain to raise strong feelings against the whole Douglas family – Moray included. And where would his chance of the Regency be then?"

Lindsay backed down, muttering, before this tirade, but the Old Lady was relentless. "And besides all that," she added, "neither I nor any of my family is the monster of cruelty *you* are, my lord." The look that had pinned Lindsay shifted, and transfixed Ruthven instead. "*Or* a snake in the grass like you, my lord."

Ruthven tried, but failed, to outface her; and had to content himself with a mutter that no-one could distinguish. I wanted to laugh, then. There was no-one so formidable as the Old Lady when she was in her stride. And yet, I thought, that was partly why I was as fond of her as she was of me. She, at least, was never dull when she was quenching people with that glare and flicking the acid of her tongue at them!

George was on his feet by that time, knowing well that he was the one who would be chosen to ride to

Edinburgh; and within minutes of this, I was rowing him over to the New House stables. I got back to the island landing-stage to find Ellen and Margaret waiting there for me. They helped me beach the boat, chattering all the time of the Queen and George's mission to Edinburgh – but not a word, I noticed, of Lindsay's part in the scene before George departed.

I chattered with them, aware of Ellen's tact in avoiding this – for Margaret's sake, of course – but without much patience, myself, for the girl. She was old enough now, after all, to take her father's failings for granted – just as I did, for instance, where Sir William was concerned.

"The Queen's physician," Ellen informed me, "is a Frenchman. That is because she prefers to have French servants. The Old Lady said so. And her cook is French too. He is a Provençal, by the name of Diderot. And the physician, the Old Lady said, is called Arnault – M'sieur Claude Arnault."

Ellen was good at picking up information! I went back to my duties, turning these scraps over in my mind and deciding it could very well be useful to strike up an acquaintance with the second of these men – this M'sieur Arnault, who would certainly be on close terms with the Queen. And to better that acquaintance, of course, if it seemed to be leading in the direction I wanted to go!

I was waiting by the gate when George returned that evening with both men in tow. The cook, I saw then, was a plump man, with a melancholy and rather handsome face; but the appearance of Arnault the physician was far from attractive. Short, swarthy-skinned, with a great stomach and a warty nose – that was how he looked. But the little eyes above the warty nose were merry ones. I liked the knowing twinkle they held; and before long, I discovered, I had developed quite a liking for the man himself.

It was in the garden I first spoke to him, beside the herb-bed at its far end. The garden itself lay outside the wall around the Castle courtyard, and stretched to take up all that part of the island not occupied by the buildings enclosed by the wall. The garden, also, was well planted with shrubs and trees, so that it was easy for me to stalk M'sieur Arnault on his herb-gathering expedition, and then to saunter casually from cover to talk to him.

The greeting I called brought him up from his stooped position at the herb-bed. He had a fistful of greenery in his hand, and waving this towards the bed, he told me,

"This is shameful, the neglect of these good plants here."

The herb-bed was certainly very weed-grown. I said defensively. "It was well looked after in the Old Lady's day."

"The Old Lady – ? Ah yes, Lady Margaret Douglas."

"She used to be Keeper of the Castle," I explained. "After she was widowed, and Sir William was still a minor. That is why he depends on her so much. And *everything* was in good order then – or so they tell me, at least. But Lady Agnes – Sir William's wife, she is – well, she is very placid. She does not much care what happens or how things look, so long as life goes on somehow."

"Herbs," Arnault retorted, "can *be* life. Herbs are the raw stuff of medicines. And I need them, just as

27

every physician does."

I jumped for the opening he had given me. With a nod to the herbs in his hand, I asked, "And your medicine from these – will that cure the Queen?"

Arnault cocked his head at me, little eyes suddenly a-glitter with sardonic humour. "That," he told me, "could be called a strange question – coming from a page. Could it not?"

I shrugged. "I do not think so. You arrived only yesterday; and the Queen was very ill then. But you do not seem too concerned now, M'sieu, and so I wondered – "

"If that fat little Frenchman really could cure her," Arnault interrupted. "And so you lay in wait for me, you followed me, and now you make a casual chance to ask me. Is that not so?"

Again I shrugged, but in admission of his charge this time, and feeling not a little embarrassed by the way he had seen through my manoeuvres. Arnault chuckled, a rich fat sound, at the sight of the flush on my face. Then, as suddenly as if he had been struck, his grin vanished. His face became lowering, dark with menace. In a voice loaded with suspicion, he asked,

"But why are you so curious, my young friend – or should I say, '*my young enemy*'? Are you another of those who wish so much that the Queen should die?"

I backed from his look stammering. "No! M'sieu Arnault, believe me, no! I am on *her* side."

Arnault looked me up and down. "You are more than page to Sir William. You are also, I believe – ahem – a Douglas by blood. And so what have you to gain by being a friend to the Queen – here, in this nest of her enemies?"

"Why, nothing," I told him. And then, with laughter beginning suddenly to bubble up in me, I added, "And everything!"

Arnault was quick to understand. "Of course, of course." He nodded, with some of the menace clearing from his face. "You have here in this Castle, a dull life. And so you look for excitement – but for its own sake only. You gain no reward; but to you, that is still everything – yes?"

"Yes. Exactly yes, M'sieu." The laughter was coming through my voice now, and I did not try to damp it down. "And if the Queen were to try to escape from here – "

"Hush!" Arnault's hand shot out to clamp over my mouth. "Do not say that word. Not yet, at least. First of all, she must be cured of this illness."

I pulled his hand from my face. "But can you do that, M'sieu? Can you?"

Arnault drew himself up as much as his fat stomach allowed. "I am a good physician," he said proudly. "With modesty, I may say, an exceedingly good physician. What is more I recognise the nature of the Queen's illness. She has had it before, I cured her then, and – with God's help – I will do so again."

I said "Amen" to this, but not with any great certainty, and Arnault noticed my lack of fervour. "I see," he remarked drily, "that you are not much given to habits of devotion. But I am, my young friend. And if you truly wish for the Queen to be well again – "

"I do, M'sieu," I interrupted. "In all truth, I assure you of that."

"Then pray for her," Arnault retorted. "As I shall! Because a word in God's ear, I must tell you, will often do more good than any medicine. And one more thing – " A fat forefinger beckoning brought me closer to himself. "That man who came here with me – Diderot, the Queen's cook; he is blindly loyal to her – you understand?"

I was not sure I did understand, but I nodded all the same, and Arnault went on, "He is also an expert with a meat-cleaver. Not that you have anything to fear from that of course, unless – " The big warty face came even closer to my own, and with warm breath hissing on my cheek, Arnault finished, " – unless I find you have played me false to-day. And then, my young friend, one word from me in Diderot's ear, and he will split you as neatly as he would split a chicken."

I stepped nervously back from him, rubbing the moist patch his breath had left on my cheek. Here was another, it seemed, who was "blindly loyal" to the Queen. And so he was still testing me out, using Diderot like a threat to frighten me. And, I realised, he had come very close to success in that! As coolly as I could then I told him,

"I am in no danger, M'sieu, from Diderot's cleaver."

Arnault's face changed swiftly again into a mask of sardonic humour; and that was when I decided I liked the man. He was not unlike myself, after all – in some respects, at least. That piece of play-acting over Diderot, for instance; that was the kind of thing *I* liked to do. There was something attractive, also, in his humour. And of course, he was as conceited as I was myself! I thought of him saying, "*With modesty ... an exceedingly good physician*," and grinned in reply as he asked,

"So I make myself clear now, do I?"

"Very clear, M'sieu."

"Good. And you will remember my advice on prayer?"

"Whenever I can, M'sieu."

Arnault was satisfied at last. "In that case," he told me, "you must also hope with me that God will not be asleep in Lochleven this summer. And meanwhile, you can bend your back to help pick these herbs, so that I can give Him what assistance I may."

5

I found it a nuisance, that promise I had given
Arnault, and my prayers for the Queen were not so
long or so frequent as they might have been. But I
did pray. And she did get well; well enough at first to
eat the delicate-flavoured concoctions Diderot prepared for her, then well enough finally to go walking
in the garden with her ladies – Jane Kennedy and
Maria de Courcelles – on either side of her.

We watched them from a little distance, Ellen and
Margaret and myself. Kennedy was a tiny creature,
no bigger than a child of twelve, but de Courcelles
was nearly as tall as the Queen herself. They looked
like two women walking with a little girl, Ellen
remarked; then she exclaimed aloud as the three of
them moved into a patch of sunlight.

It had been a miserable summer that year, and this
was one of the few fine days we had had. The sun's
rays bathed the Queen's head, making the red-gold
of her hair seem suddenly like a nimbus around it.
Margaret, too, drew a gasping breath of admiration,
and whispered to Ellen,

"I would like to see it all spread out for combing –
would you not?"

I heard the conversation that followed, without really hearing it. The Queen was walking with some of her easy, dancing grace beginning to show again in her step, and that was a pleasant sight. It would have been a reassuring one too, I thought, if I had not known that Lindsay and Ruthven had already begun to plague her daily for the promise they wanted. And how could she get really well when that was happening?

She was holding them both at bay with argument. Arnault had told me so. He had also told me how much these arguments exhausted her. And in addition to all that now, of course, there was this new emissary from the lords – this man, Sir Robert Melville, who had begun to travel back and forth between them and the Queen.

I was curious about the same Sir Robert. He had a foppish appearance, certainly – all ringlets and ribbons and laces and high-heeled shoes. In his manner, also, he was more like some fool of a dancing-master than the skilled politician he was supposed to be. But his face...! There now, we were into a different matter! The face, I was sure, was that of a clever man – thin-featured, long-lipped, with languid-drooping eyelids that most successfully veiled the shrewdness behind them.

I wondered who I could ask about him. Minny was not acquainted with the circles where men like Sir Robert moved. Nor was Arnault of any help, except to tell me that the Queen had held several private conversations with Sir Robert. There was nothing for it, I realised, except to be even more than usually observant when he visited; and was finally rewarded for my pains in this when I saw him one day in the garden, deep in conversation with George.

They were talking secretly. From the watchful looks they cast around them, I was sure of that. I began looking for a chance to coax George into telling me something of their conversation; but that chance had still to come my way when I discovered that God had been asleep in Lochleven, after all, that summer.

It was Arnault who proclaimed it so; Arnault with every line of his body drooping, the light gone from his eyes, face haggard, the step that carried him into the Great Hall no more than a shamble. He gave his news briefly, ignoring all the others there, and speaking direct to Sir William.

The Queen had fallen ill again; but not, this time, with the feverish malady that had previously attacked her. This time, Arnault said, the Queen's illness was due to the fact that she had miscarried of her child.

I watched him as he stood there, small and fat in his black gown, yet with the sorrow in his face making him somehow dignified. What reception would he find for the news that had moved *him* so deeply? My mind went back to the conversation I had overheard on the day the Queen was brought to the island, and I feared for the little man. Sir William spoke, awkwardly, his face embarrassed.

"You may – er – tell Her Grace that I – er – send her my commiserations."

"Commiserations?" That was Ruthven, slyly, a mocking smile flashing out with the word.

"Aye, be damned to such talk!" Lindsay exclaimed. "The brat was Bothwell's. And now that this has happened, it is just as Ruthven said it would be. One complication, at least, has been removed from the scene."

I looked at the Old Lady, waiting for her to blast them as she had done on the last occasion they talked so unfeelingly; but the Old Lady only shrugged, and said,

"It *is* a problem solved, of course. And we should be grateful for that."

I gaped at her words. Was this what power, and the craving for power did to people? The Old Lady *loved* children – who knew that better than I? – yet here she was now, talking of the death of a child as casually as she would have spoken of a discarded pawn on a chess board!

"I will inform Her Grace of your opinions." That was Arnault again, but speaking this time in a voice that carried a quiet and deadly hatred. "And meanwhile, if you will excuse me..." He turned to Sir William. "I must ask your permission to leave, sir. I – I find myself suddenly unwell."

"M'sieu, I regret – er –" Sir William was immediately all flustered concern. In a flurry of words he granted Arnault's request, and hurriedly added, "My page will escort you."

I saw George's eyes on Arnault as I armed the little man from the Hall, and was half-expecting it when I heard him following swiftly behind the two of us. The tremble I had felt when I gripped Arnault's arm was still there; but it was rage that shook him, I guessed, rather than the illness he had claimed, and so I had not dared speak to him. Neither had he spoken to me by the time George caught up on our progress across the courtyard; but from George himself, the words were tumbling.

"M'sieu! M'sieu Arnault! Not all of us here are

35

savages. I pray you, M'sieu, to believe that, and to tell Her Grace how heartily sorry I am for her misfortune."

Arnault straightened, shaking my hand from his arm. He stared at George. Then he nodded, a curt little nod, and said,

"I am your good servant, M'sieu Douglas."

The service had been softly spoken, I noticed, in spite of the curtness of the nod; and as Arnault turned and walked from us, I was glad of the comfort George's words must have given him. On impulse, I said,

"I wish *I* had thought of sending such a message."

"You?" George looked his disbelief at me. "You never cared for anyone in your life – except yourself!"

The thought of Minny flashed into my mind. "That is not true," I said resentfully. "Not entirely, anyway."

"I am sorry, Will." George looked away from me, biting his lip. "I had forgotten Minny. This whole business of the Queen, you see – it upsets my mind so that I cannot think properly."

Abruptly he turned towards the outbuilding that held the mews for the hawks he was so fond of training. My resentment slid from me. I caught his arm and quickly asked,

"Does it upset you enough to discuss it with Sir Robert Melville?"

"How do you – ? You were *spying* on me!"

George had more than his share of the temper that ran in the Douglas family. I backed from him as he struck at my clutching hand and furiously accused me.

"Wait, George, wait," I begged. "I did spy on

you. I admit that. But only to see if I could find out what sort of man Melville is – whether he is friend to the Queen, or foe. Because *I* am on her side, George. And I will help her if I can."

George stared at me. With a jerk of his head then, he commanded me to follow him towards the mews; and there, between the fluttering lines of his perched hawks, he faced me again.

"Did you mean what you said about the Queen?" he asked. 'Truly mean it?"

I nodded. "Yes. I am quite decided on that."

"Why? Why should *you* want to help her?"

"Because –" I stopped there, with my mouth open on the same answer I had given Arnault. What would a man of George's noble character think if I gave my true reason for wanting to take a hand in the Queen's affairs? My mind raced, working on all the possibilities.

I wanted George to trust me, as Minny did. I had always wanted that. But I had worked to earn Minny's trust; and if I lied to George now . . .

"You are very slow to answer." He was watching me, his face suspicious. I called up all my courage, and told him,

"For the excitement of it. Because it will make life here less dull for me."

George shrugged and turned away to gentle the bird perched nearest him. "That sounds like you," he remarked; and his tone was so disparaging that I blurted out,

"And also because she was kind to me. When I was only a small boy –" I stopped, feeling foolish over what I had been about to say. George glanced at me over his shoulder, and quietly urged,

"Go on, Will."

"She – she disliked to hear those who jeered 'bastard' at me. Remember? She had her own name for me. '*My little orphan*' – that was what she called me. You remember that too – do you not, George?"

"I remember," George said. And then, speaking low as if to himself, he added, "I remember too much about her, I think, for my own comfort."

"George –" I ventured a touch on his shoulder. "About Melville. *Is* he her friend?"

George turned full towards me and said, "Give me one good reason why I should tell you anything about Melville."

"I have given you one already," I protested. "I want to help the Queen. And – and you can trust me, George."

"Can I?" George came closer with this; close enough to peer into my face. Softly then, he added, "You are a liar, Will. You know you are."

"I admit that." My heart was hammering by this time. I could hear the unsteadiness in my own voice. Yet still I knew I had to convince George there and then, or never have his trust at all. And so I pushed myself on to tell him, "But I spoke the truth about myself to you just now, when I could have pretended to some nobler reason for wanting to help the Queen. I always will do that, I promise you. And I will never, never repeat anything you might tell me."

There was a long moment of silence between us; a very long moment. Then George said, "I believe you."

I found myself grinning – foolishly grinning, no doubt, such a shock of pleasure went through me then; but I sobered quickly enough when George said,

"About Melville, then. Outwardly, he is working on behalf of the lords; but in secret, he *is* the Queen's friend. And, he says, she must be persuaded to sign that Deed of Abdication. There is no way of keeping her life safe otherwise. And so he has concocted a plan to defeat this situation. Also, he has smuggled in to her various tokens that the plan will succeed – pledges of support from some of the lords still faithful to her, along with a letter from the English Ambassador, written at the direct command of the Queen of England."

I let out such a whistle of surprise at this, that all the hawks were startled from their perches. George frowned annoyance at me, but once he had the birds quiet again, he went on,

"That letter told the Queen something which is perfectly true. A signature obtained under duress has no legal force; and it also reminded her that there is no power on earth which can take away her natural-born right to be Queen. Therefore, the English Queen urged, our Queen should sign the Deed. But only in order to safeguard her life. And afterwards, she will have every right to repudiate the signature."

"Afterwards?"

"After she escapes from here."

I stared at George. "Is Melville planning that too?"

George grinned – a very wry grin – and said, "Not he! Melville has sympathy enough for the Queen; but he is still the kind who always waits to see which way the cat will jump. And until he can tell whether it is to be the Queen or the lords who will finally triumph, he would not so far commit himself."

"But he thinks you will!"

"He thinks I might." George corrected, "and that was why he decided to sound me out on the matter. I have made no secret, after all, of my distress at the Queen's situation. And he knows perfectly well that she is more likely to sign the Deed if he can hold out to her even a hope of escaping afterwards."

"And will you, George – will you help her escape?"

George turned his back on me, making no answer. I gave him a moment, and then repeated, "Will you, George?"

"Oh, for pity's sake!" He whirled towards me again. "Lochleven is a State Prison and *my brother* is its hereditary Keeper! Or had you forgotten all that? It would be stark ruin for him if *I* helped the Queen escape."

I stood in silence, trying to imagine myself in George's shoes. Would I betray a brother for the sake of the Queen? And there was something else George had not mentioned – some *one* else, rather. Moray. His half-brother! If the Queen abdicated or died, and Moray became Regent, George's fortunes would soar along with those of the other Douglases. But if George tried to help the Queen escape, and was caught in this, he would face the powerful vengeance Moray could bring on him.

"You said you wanted to help," George broke into my thoughts. "And you can. Melville comes here again tomorrow, bringing the Deed with him; and he is convinced he can persuade the Queen to sign then – provided I am at hand to reassure her afterwards – "

"But you said – "

"I said nothing! And I said nothing to Melville either, except that I agreed he could tell the Queen I would stand her friend in any way I could. And so, when Melville arrives along with his two witnesses to the signing – two of the legal gentlemen they call Notaries Public – what I want *you* to do is to act as messenger for any meeting he might arrange between the Queen and myself. Do you agree to that?"

"With all my heart," I told him.

George smiled a little at the warmth of my reply, but was immediately serious again as he warned,

"And remember your promise. Not a word of all this to *anyone.*"

I was about to give a very ordinary sort of assurance to this when I thought of a phrase that had a fine, heroic ring to it – the sort of phrase, it seemed to me, that could very well have been put into a play. I spoke my phrase aloud.

"I shall wear silence like a shield!"

I said this, I believe, in the grand manner suited to it; but all it drew from George was the kind of look I was more accustomed to receiving from the Old Lady.

"There are times," he told me, "when you talk just like a play-actor."

I decided to ignore the look and treat the remark as the compliment it should have been. George and I, after all, were now fellow-conspirators – were we not? My only reply, therefore, was to sweep him a bow, with a very elegant angle to my right leg and a fine flourish of my hands. But this had the effect of again startling the hawks; and, irritably, as he went once more to soothe them, George threw over his shoulder at me,

"And behave just like one too."

I bowed again, making such a comical caper of this second bow, that George laughed in spite of himself.

"I know that," I told him. "But you must admit,

George, that I have a considerable talent for it."

"Why d'ye call it a talent?" he demanded. "You make a fool of yourself, behaving so."

"I know that also." I had realised by then that I was about to reveal more of my secret self than I usually did; but by that time also, the exhilaration of having George's trust at last had gone to my head, and so I could not stop myself. "But one thing *you* do not know, George, is that clowning like this is a good way of hiding what is really in my mind. And that is something I have always found very useful!"

George looked at me in a puzzled sort of way. "So long as you remember," he said, "that clowning will not help the Queen."

"How can you tell that?" I asked. "The most dangerous of situations, George, can be disguised in laughter. And that means the Queen may yet have need of a Court Jester!"

6

I took my leave of George with this, still grinning at the way I had tied up his tongue with my arguments. I was not nearly so light-hearted, however, as I waited with him the next day at the landing-stage to meet Sir Robert arriving with his Notaries Public.

They were like two draggled rooks flanking a peacock, I thought, looking at the contrast between his finery and their lawyers' gowns of shabby black. But their eyes were cold, their faces grim, and I did not care for the probing glances they gave me when George drew Sir Robert aside to speak privately to him.

I turned away from their looks, to see George walking off towards the garden and Sir Robert beckoning me towards himself. I closed with him, and he spoke low and rapidly to me.

"I have been assured I can trust you; and the plan is this. I must have time alone with the Queen; and so take these Notaries to Sir William. Get from him the key to the Queen's tower. Remind him it *was* agreed I should see the Queen in private before he joins me here with the lords Ruthven and Lindsay. Do not let either of these two see you. And come quickly back with that key!"

A signal of his hand brought the Notaries to him. "Go with this page," he instructed; and immediately I began urging them across the courtyard, hurrying them along like a collie herding sheep. A few minutes of this was enough to exhaust my patience. I pointed ahead, and said,

"D'you see that flight of steps built against the Castle's outer wall? It leads to the level of the second floor; and the doorway at the top of the steps is the chief entrance to the Castle. It gives directly on to the Great Hall. And I will ask Sir William to meet you there."

I was off then, without giving either a chance to protest. I took the outer stair in a series of bounds, stepped through the Hall doorway, then ducked sharply on to all fours. Facing me, as I crouched like this, and about four feet inside the doorway, was the screen we called the "service screen" – solid wood in its lower half, lattice work above that. I crawled forward and peered through the lattice. Lindsay was in the Hall, and Ruthven; but not Sir William. I ducked again, and considered my next hazard.

On my left, in the south-eastern corner of the Hall, was the only way of reaching Sir William's apartments – the wheel-stair that twisted downwards to the kitchen and upwards to all the floors above the level of the Hall. But the screen did not stretch the full breadth of the Hall. There was a gap between it and the south wall – the necessary gap that allowed entrance to the main body of the Hall. I started towards the stair, crawling along behind the solid lower half of the screen. At the extremity of this cover, I paused to eye the space ahead of me.

If I moved fast enough, I decided, Lindsay and

Ruthven might not be aware of me flashing towards the stair. I judged my distance, balanced myself, and rose in a cat-like leap that carried me on to the fourth step. As silently as I had leapt, then, I raced upwards to the level of Sir William's apartments, and entered hurriedly on my own knock at his door.

Sir William was there, close in conversation with the Old Lady. The speed of my entrance took them by surprise, and they started apart with something that looked very like guilt on their faces. I rattled off my message, told Sir William where he would find the Notaries, and held out my hand for the key. Sir William began fumbling it off his belt, talking as he did so, in the flustered manner that always overcame him when he was embarrassed.

"Yes. Ah yes, Will. But I – um – I – You must – er – tell Sir Robert that I myself shall not be present when the – um – lords Lindsay and Ruthven go to speak to Her Grace."

"That a matter of importance to be attended to here will not allow of that." Quickly, smoothly, the Old Lady came in on Sir William's stumbled excuse. Much too quickly, I thought. And much too smoothly!

I thought again of the guilty looks while I repeated my manoeuvres for passing unseen by Lindsay and Ruthven; and raced back to Sir Robert feeling certain I knew what lay behind those looks. The pair of them had been planning that Sir William would deliberately absent himself from the lords' interview with the Queen. But why? My guess at the answer to this frightened me, and I ran all the faster.

I found Sir Robert striding back and forth at the Queen's tower, ribbons and laces all a-flutter in the wind of his impatience. I handed over the key, blurting out as I did so,

"Sir William has excused himself from the interview between the Queen and the lords; and I can
guess why. He has never cared to be mixed up in violence, and he does not want to witness what might
happen then. Because you know how violent Lord
Lindsay can be."

There was no veiling of Sir Robert's eyes now.
They were wide and alert, bright with calculation.
"There will be no call for anyone to use violence," he
told me. "Not if I have this time alone with the
Queen." Still speaking, he turned to unlock the
door. "But I must still have you close at hand when
the moment comes to fetch Mr Douglas. And so
come on, lad."

I hung back, not yet convinced. "But sir – What if
the Queen will not agree to your plan? What if she
will not sign the Deed? Should I not warn Mr
Douglas now that there could be danger to her?"

"The Queen will sign. She has a subtle nature, and
it is the very subtlety of my plan that will appeal to
her." Sir Robert had started up the stairs inside the
tower, with this; and, calling back as he continued
towards the Queen's chamber, he added, "So do as
you are told, instead of wasting precious time here in
argument."

I followed him up the stairs, still feeling uneasy,
but reassured by one thing at least. Whatever else he
had agreed to with Lindsay and Ruthven, Sir
William would never countenance murder. And so
the Queen's life was not really in danger. What was
more, I argued, if I ran for George now I would be
forcing him to a decision he had seemed unwilling to
make. And he certainly would not thank me for that!

Sir Robert knocked on the door of the Queen's

chamber, and a voice bade him enter. I slid in on his heels, louting low in her presence, as he did. Arnault was in the chamber with her, along with Kennedy and de Courcelles; and she herself was lying in bed, propped up on a great pile of pillows.

Everything about her was white – the pillows themselves, her bedgown, the cover and hangings of the bed; and the great mass of her hair was spread out against this whiteness in a wide and shining web of copper-gold. Her eyes travelled from Sir Robert to rest on my face.

"Will Douglas?" She spoke then, uncertainly, her voice questioning – because I had grown, of course, in the two years since she had seen me. I opened my mouth to answer; but before I could do so, she smiled and said, "Yes, it is. It *is* my little orphan!"

I bowed again, in a confusion of surprise and pleasure. She had remembered her name for me. Even in the midst of all this, she had remembered it!

Sir Robert had moved to the bed, and was quietly offering his sympathy on the loss of her child. But his face was anxious; and very soon, he was bending down to speak in an even quieter voice. The Queen answered him in French, the language always readiest to her tongue, and he continued in French also. I could make out little of what they said. My schooling had made me fluent enough in French, but those low tones defeated me. I stopped trying to listen, and watched their faces instead. Sir Robert's anxiety was still obvious; and who could blame him for that? He would be a famous figure, after all, if his plan succeeded; disgraced, if it was discovered. And if it failed altogether... The Queen, I noticed, kept interrupting his speech, her face vivid with anger sometimes, and sometimes downcast. She used her hands a lot as she talked, long white hands with round-tipped fingers that were as expressive as her face. Her voice rose in volume until at last I clearly heard her say,

" – and you take from me my only weapon, if I sign. Consider also, Melville, I am an anointed Queen. It goes against God, therefore, as well as against nature for me to strip myself of my Royal rights."

Melville's voice also rose. "God is all-seeing, Your Grace, and the signing is only a device ﹐to protect your life for the day you will regain your throne. It will not be considered a sin in you to use any stratagem to that end."

The Queen sighed, a great deep sigh. It was her only answer to this last argument, and I thought, "*She is wavering.*" Abruptly then, she said,

"If it is true, what you have told me of George Douglas, I must see him immediately this business is over."

"Then you *will* sign, Your Grace?" Sir Robert straightened, relief beginning to smooth the worry from his face. Her hands fluttered in another of those expressive gestures.

"You are right. I was born a Queen. Nothing can ever make me less. And once I am free again . . ."

Sir Robert bent quickly in the gesture of kissing her hand, and in the very moment of his doing so, the door of her chamber was burst roughly open. Lindsay strode in, with Ruthven and the two Notaries at his heels. Lindsay's voice rang out, the gesture that went with the words taking in Arnault and the two *femmes de chambre*.

"Out!" he roared. "Out of here, all of you!" They backed in confusion from him, Arnault scowling, the two young women in a flutter of distress, and withdrew into the inner chamber of the Queen's apartments. Lindsay glared down at the Queen. "Now," he told her grimly, "we will have no interruptions with women weeping and that damned physician of yours speaking above his station."

He had not noticed me thus far. Either that, or he meant to ignore my presence. He was accustomed, after all, to see me stand waiting to be sent running with this or that message. I stayed where I was – in a far corner of the room with my back pressed to the wall. Lindsay turned to the Notaries.

"The Deed," he commanded. From inside his black gown, one of the Notaries produced a long roll of yellow parchment. From inside *his* gown, the other Notary produced a pen and an inkwell. Their gestures were so polished, so smooth with practice, that they were like a pair of conjurors performing sleight of hand. Lindsay snatched the Deed, and threw it down before the Queen.

"The law demands that you know the exact contents of the Deed," he told her; "and we mean to observe the law. You will read it aloud, therefore; every word of it."

The Queen had drawn herself up to sit very erect. "You will find yourself hard put to it to observe the law in this case, my lord," she said tartly; "because *I will not read that Deed*. And furthermore, I will not sign it."

Sir Robert began to exclaim in dismay, but the sound he made was over-topped by Lindsay roaring at him,

"You told us, Melville! You smooth-tongued viper, you! You told us you could persuade her to sign!"

"And I did, I did!" Reproachfully, Sir Robert turned to the Queen. "Your Grace, what is this? You agreed to sign."

"Yes, indeed," the Queen retorted. "I did agree – but that was before the sight of Lord Lindsay reminded me of the kind of men to whom that would have given my kingdom."

Ruthven and Sir Robert both began speaking, at this; but Lindsay's uplifted hands silenced them. "I have the best answer to that," he told them. He stepped close to the bed, and bent towards the Queen. "Rise up," he ordered. "If you will not sign, I am ordered to take you to a place where –" He stopped, as if measuring the power of his next words, and then finished, " – *where I can give a good account of you!*"

There was no mistaking the menace of these last words. They were a death-threat, if ever I heard one. But the Queen did not flinch from them. Bluntly, she told him,

"I am sick. I cannot rise."

"You mean you will not!"

"No. I cannot. But I would not if I could."

I have never seen a man look so baffled as Lindsay did then – nor a woman so determined as the Queen. She had won that round, I thought; because – short of dragging her forcibly from her bed – how could Lindsay meet such an answer? Ruthven came forward to pluck at Lindsay's sleeve, and then to whisper in his ear. Lindsay nodded. Ruthven went to whisper to one of the Notaries. The Notary nodded, and sidled towards the Queen's bed. The Deed lay where it had fallen in front of her. She had not deigned to lay so much as a finger on it.

Nervously, like a hard-mouthed dog bringing off

a bad retrieve, the Notary snatched it up, unrolled it, and began to read aloud. The Queen closed her eyes. Her face smoothed of all expression, she lay back against her pillows. The droning voice of the Notary continued – interminably, it seemed to me. I did not understand a fraction of the legal jargon of it all, but the reading did end at last.

"There!" Delicately Ruthven took the Deed from the Notary's hands, and laid it again before the Queen. Where the Notary's actions had been awkward, his were smooth, insinuating; like those of a snake gliding into a good position for a strike. "We have observed the law, Your Grace, in spite of you. And you now know the contents of the Deed."

"And which, in spite of all you have said," Lindsay added, "you will now sign."

The Queen's eyes flew open. Her breath had begun to come hard. A patch of feverish-bright colour had appeared high on either cheek-bone. With one hand she swept the Deed off the bed, and at the same time cried,

"I will not sign. Before God, my lord, I swear that to you!"

"And before God, I swear to *you*, Madam! I am not willing to cut your throat; but if you do not sign, you compel me to it!"

Lindsay's hand travelled to his scabbard as he spoke. There was the whistling noise of steel against steel as his sword leapt free. The Queen screamed, a long shrill note of terror; and with arm extended towards her, the naked blade making a quivering line of light between them, Lindsay roared.

"You will sign. Or I will kill you."

"Never." She managed the word in the faintest of voices. And then, on a stronger, rising note, in her accustomed French, *"Jamais! Jamais de ma vie!"*

The room was all confusion by then, with Sir Robert scrabbling on his knees for the Deed, Arnault and the Queen's two ladies rushing in from the inner apartment, the Notaries cowering back as far as they could from Lindsay; and with myself – all indecision now ended – sidling towards the door so that I could go dashing for George Douglas. In the midst of all this, also, I was aware of Ruthven throwing himself on his knees beside the bed. His face white as porridge, he babbled as he knelt,

"In the name of Christ, Madam, I beg you to sign. *I* do not wish you dead; but he lies – Lindsay lies when he says he is not willing to kill you."

The Queen paid no heed to Ruthven, or to anyone else there. Her gaze was fixed on the point of Lindsay's sword-blade, and she was pressing as far back from it as she could. With every fraction her pillows yielded, the sword-point travelled nearer. It was aimed at her throat. Lindsay's face above it was bloated and purple with rage, his eyes glittered supernaturally bright; but the hand gripping the sword-hilt was rock-steady.

At the back of my mind I heard a voice saying over and over, *"He cannot kill her now – not in front of all these witnesses."* But Lindsay looked mad. At that moment, he *was* mad. He could, he *would* kill her. The shock of this realisation held me like one paralysed, and the others there seemed to be similarly held. We were like a roomful of statues – except for Lindsay. His right arm was still moving; slowly, surely bringing the sword-point closer to the Queen's throat.

She could go no further back from it. Motionless, eyes wide open and glazed with terror, she pressed against her pillows. The sword-point was two inches from her throat.

"Sign," The single word came from Lindsay with a rumbling, grating sound.

"No." Her lips scarcely moving, she answered it.

"Sign." The sword was an inch from her.

"No." Her answer this time was little more than a sigh.

The sword-point touched her throat. She screamed again; and the sound was like a signal of release for the frozen horror in the room. All three of her attendants started towards her. Sir Robert thrust the Deed in front of her. With shaking hands that spattered ink all over it, he offered her a pen. Her right hand closed on the pen. Lindsay swung his sword up and away from her. With her left hand, then, she took the handkerchief Arnault offered her, and pressed it to the place where the sword had rested. Lindsay stood looking down at her, the congested blood draining from his face, his eyes taking on a more normal appearance.

"I will say this," he told her, "there is much courage in you."

Instantly she flung back at him, "But less in you, my lord, to threaten where it should be your duty to protect."

I thought Lindsay would explode then, into another bout of manic fury; but I was wrong. He looked at her, apparently dumbfounded by the way she had so swiftly gone back to the offensive; and almost querulously, he asked,

"Why do you parley with me? In God's name, why? You know we have you in a corner."

Her hand, the right hand holding the pen, went disdainfully wide of the Deed. "Would you not parley, my lord, if you had as much at stake as I?"

She was going to fight it out to the bitter end, I realised – perhaps even to a further threat on her life; and meanwhile, one of the Notaries was immovably blocking the doorway, which meant there was no way I could get out to fetch George. I edged nearer the door, hearing the continued debate going on between Lindsay and the Queen, but no longer listening to it. If there was only some way I could make that Notary move...! But the fellow seemed fixed as a rock.

I watched him as intently as he was watching the Queen and Lindsay, his eyes going back and forward from one to the other, his whole face showing how fascinated he was by the argument between them. And the Queen seemed so endlessly ready to twist and turn in search of some way out of signing that Deed! I began to despair of the whole situation. But there was one factor in it that I had forgotten. The Queen was sick. And she was so near now to the end of her reserves that her strength could no longer match her will. Her head drooped. Her hand fell to the paper. Almost fainting, she scrawled her name.

"I sign this –" Brokenly she spoke, as her hand went through its motions, " – under protest." The pen dropped from her hand. "I shall repudiate this signature – " Her eyes met those of Lindsay. " – the moment I am free to do so."

"You will never be free." Lindsay snatched up the Deed and stood towering over her. "You swore to have my head. But I shall make sure the Privy Council acts swiftly on this Deed. And then we will see whose head will roll!"

I did not hear what followed this. In the few seconds since the Queen had signed, the Notary blocking the doorway had moved nearer the bed. As Lindsay spoke, I was easing the door open; and seconds later I was running like the wind, calling for George as I entered the garden, and not caring in the least who heard me do so.

George came running to meet me. I beckoned him on, then turned in my tracks and ran back to the tower. George's longer strides caught up with mine. We ran side by side, with me gasping out my tale as we ran. Then George drew ahead of me. I caught up with him again outside the door to the Queen's chamber, where he stood saying fiercely to Sir Robert,

"You have mis-managed this, Melville. You should have had my brother here to restrain Lindsay."

There was nothing suave or elegant about Sir Robert now. His figure sagged, as if something inside of him had broken. The lines of his face were twisted. With his laces and ribbons all drooping from that sagging body he looked, in fact, like a puppet-eer's doll with its strings slackened.

"But Mr Douglas," he faltered, "it was Sir William's own decision not to be present."

"Then you should have insisted otherwise," George retorted; and pushed brusquely past him into the Queen's chamber.

She was lying back against her pillows. Only Arnault and the waiting-ladies were in the room with her now. Her face was as white as the white of her bed. Her eyes were closed. And she lay so still that – except for the gleaming mass of her hair – she could have been a white marble angel on a tomb of white marble. I checked my step, as transfixed by the sight as George was. And then the marble angel bled!

From the white, slender column of throat above the coverlet, a globule of blood welled darkly, broke, and trickled downwards in a thin crawl of scarlet. Arnault exclaimed in anger, and stepped forward with a piece of linen in his hand; but George was even quicker to move. On one knee beside the bed, he watched as Arnault's linen checked the bleeding. In a whisper, Arnault told him,

"Be easy, M'sieu. Her Grace bleeds freely from any wound. And Lindsay's sword did no more than scratch her skin."

George nodded, but his face was still anxious. Arnault stepped back at last, satisfied with his effort. George stayed where he was, his face on the level with that of the Queen. Her eyes opened. Their wide, golden-brown gaze was trance-like, at first. It rested on George, and recognition took over from the tranced look.

"Mr Douglas." She spoke slowly, and very faintly.

"Your Grace." George's answering voice was firm, but I could see the tremble in the hand he had laid beside her own on the coverlet. "Tell me, Your Grace, how I can serve you."

"Lindsay – " she managed. "He said – he said he would take me from here to some secret place. He means to – to murder me."

"No, Your Grace. Not while I am alive to prevent that!"

Her eyes fixed full on George. "I must be set free," she said; "publicly set free, so that I may clear my name of the slanders on it. That is the only way to undo my situation now."

"Command me then, Your Grace," George answered gently. "Tell me your will."

The Queen stayed silent a moment, as if gathering her strength; and when she spoke again, her voice gained speed and urgency with every word.

"Moray – my brother Moray. He had no part in the rebellion. He was in France at the time. But the lords will make him Regent now; and he must not, must *not* agree to that. Will you go to him, Mr Douglas? And will you beg him to come and see me? Will you tell him I am relying now for my freedom on *his* influence with these rebellious lords?"

I stood watching the dismay gather in George's face as she spoke. This was the test he had tried to avoid; the test between chivalry to her, and his own natural loyalty to the family cause. But how was it possible, I wondered, for her to be so deceived in Moray when even such as I knew the strength of the man's ambition? How *could* she place such hopes on him when his rise to power could be achieved only through her own downfall? George, I guessed, was struggling with the same questions.

"Your Grace," he pointed out, "if my lord Moray had wanted to help you, he could easily have been here by this time."

"He does not know how I am treated!" The Queen's answering voice was a cry of anguish. "He cannot know, or he would never have permitted it. He loves me, Mr Douglas. My brother loves me!"

The Queen's hands had become as agitated with this as her voice. George reached out and took one of those restless hands in his own. He looked intently at her; and she, with tears in her eyes, looked back at him. She was beautiful always, but with those great tear-glittered eyes now, she was heart-rendingly so. In a voice so low I barely caught the words, George told her,

"Majesty, sweet Majesty, I cannot see you so distressed! I will take your message to Moray. And if *he* fails you, I swear to you now, *I* will still stand your friend in any way that will once more make you my true and only Sovereign."

A flicker of some emotion I could not name ran across her carven-pale features. Still without taking her eyes off George's face, she raised her free hand to him. He bowed his head and kissed the tips of its long white fingers. With equal gentleness, then, he kissed the fingers of her other hand.

The pact was sealed. George had finally committed himself to be now and forever the Queen's man. I was moved to see this happen – with pleasure for her, a certain apprehension for him; and for myself... I was not sure of the feeling I had on my own behalf then, but it felt remarkably like envy of George.

7

I had news the next afternoon that both surprised and dismayed me. The Queen was to be transferred to the main tower of the Castle, to the suite of rooms on the floor directly above the Great Hall; and two soldiers were to be placed daily on guard outside the door of her new lodging. That was the surprising part of the news. Dismay came when I learned the names of the soldiers chosen for the guard – Kerr, and Newland, two of the most ill-natured fellows in the barracks, and both of them also sworn enemies of the Queen.

It was Ellen who told me of the new arrangement – an Ellen whose face was all alight with excitement and an air of smugness that warned me there was more yet to be said. Ellen, I knew, was a great believer in saving the icing on her cake for the last bite!

"You are lying," I told her calmly; and instantly she rose to the bait.

"I am *not* lying, Will Douglas! These are my father's orders, and it was the Old Lady who told me so."

"Very well." I shrugged, affecting only a passing interest. "What else do you know?"

"A lot more than you think! I know that the Queen is to have all writing materials taken from her, and that she is to be watched night and day. And Will – " Ellen's rosy-fair face flushed an even deeper pink with excitement. " – it is my mother who is to sit with her by day; but at night, it is Margaret Lindsay and I who will keep watch. We are to live in the new lodgings too, and to sleep there, *in the Queen's own bed-chamber!*"

I stared in astonished disbelief. "Did the Old Lady – ?"

"Yes, she did. *'Children also can be spies.'* That was what she said to us." Ellen grinned triumphantly at me. "And that is what Margaret and I have to do now – to spy at night on the Queen's every move, so that we can tell the Old Lady whenever she does something that might mean she is planning an escape."

An escape... But what chance would there be of that now? I stared blankly at Ellen, remembering how calm Sir William and the Old Lady had remained when George told them of his mission to Moray, and realising at last the reason for this. It had not needed George, after all, to point out that public opinion would sooner or later force Moray to visit the Queen of his own accord. Yet even so, the mere fact that George was carrying the Queen's message to him must have made them suspect his further intentions. And this was their answer, this new strictness with the Queen...

"You have not congratulated me," Ellen challenged. She was watching me closely – entering already on her role of spy, I thought uneasily; and immediately began to cover myself with a pretence of jeering at her for a country girl who would not know how to behave before the Queen. But nothing, it seemed, could dent Ellen's complacency then.

"You are just jealous," she told me, "because *I* will be at the heart of all that happens now. And you are still where you were at the beginning – only on the fringe of things!"

That was a shrewd hit on Mistress Ellen's part; a very shrewd hit. But I would prove her wrong yet, I vowed. I would prove her very wrong. But first of all, I would have to make a chance to speak to George before he left with that message.

"I'll take you ashore, George," I offered, "and help you to saddle up at the New House."

The Old Lady looked up sharply. "*You* have become very helpful all of a sudden," she remarked. "And very anxious to hang around George's neck too, I notice."

"Leave him be, madam," George told her. "I shall be glad of his help."

I felt her eyes on my back as we went out together, and under my breath I said, "She misses nothing, that one!"

"She is afraid," George said. "The Queen is boxed up tight now, and yet still the great fear is that she will somehow escape and overturn that Deed of Abdication."

"If you have plans for that," I ventured, "if you *do* have plans, George, those soldiers at her door are going to be a problem for you."

George nodded. "I have thought of that. And I can see a way to counter it. But first of all, I must make contact with her supporters on the mainland. And even then, Will, my plan – *any* plan of escape – must wait until after Moray visits her. You heard how she spoke of him; how convinced she is that he will help her. And she herself will not consider escape until that hope is dead."

We had reached the landing-stage by then. As he helped me push a boat out, George added, "And the closer the Queen is held meantime of course, the less likely it is that harm can come to her – which is something to be grateful for, is it not?"

I pulled off from the shore, considering this, and was suddenly struck by the answer to Ellen's jeering that I was still only on the fringe of things. It would be quite easy for me to coax that dear silly little half-sister of mine to chatter about everything that went on in the Queen's apartments. I might even be able to persuade Margaret Lindsay to talk, nervous as she was. And Lady Agnes Douglas, of course, was such a kind-hearted, placid sort of woman. I should not have much problem there in getting snippets of information to add to the watching brief I could keep while George was away. Then there was the pattern of the soldiers' duties, the timing of the meals sent up to the Queen's apartments – everything I learned in that line might eventually prove useful to George's plan for her escape...

I found myself slipping as easily into the role of spy as Ellen seemed to have done, and was much amused at first to realise how much her smugness had been dented by the realities of her task.

"I am not sure now that we should be there at all," she confessed to me. "The Queen, you see, is still always so kind that it – well, it shames me sometimes to know I must report on all her doings."

"And Margaret," I asked, "does she also feel like that?"

"Margaret keeps herself to herself," Ellen said, "even more than she used to. I do not know *what* she feels, Will."

I took to watching Margaret each time I escorted Sir William on his official visits to the Queen; but if Lindsay's daughter had now also been touched by the tenderness that had blossomed in Ellen, she was certainly keeping that well hidden. I seldom heard her speak, and there was never any expression at all in the thin, sallow face she kept bent down to her sewing.

Sir William began threatening to beat me for the way I seemed to be "forever idling about and staring", as he called it; but on the fifth day of George's absence from the Castle he had a letter with news that meant he could keep me busy enough. Lord Lindsay, it seemed, had made good his boast about hurrying the Council on over the Deed of Abdication. On that very day of the letter's arrival, the Queen's baby son was to be crowned King James the Sixth of Scotland. And Moray had already been appointed Regent.

I went with the rest of the family when Sir William summoned us to hear the letter read aloud. Lady Agnes listened to it with the vague smile that was usual with her when she felt matters were going well. The girls sat in awed silence. But the Old Lady, of course, was irrepressibly delighted.

"My son, the Regent." She tried the words over on her tongue, and crowed with pleasure at the sound of them. Sir William beamed at her with answering pleasure.

"My brother, the Regent!" he responded. And then, as if the words had been the spark for an ex-

63

plosion of energy in him, he jumped to his feet with the first of a long string of orders for the way he meant to celebrate the news.

There was to be a bonfire in the courtyard, fireworks to be set off at the height of the bonfire, salvoes of cannon to be fired from the Castle walls; and all of it had to be ready for that evening. I was sent running immediately with his first instruction for all this; and after that, he kept me so constantly employed on his preparations that I had hardly a moment to think my own thoughts about it all.

It did cross my mind, all the same, that it was most unfeeling of him to have such a celebration with the Queen so close at hand to witness it; and when he sent me that evening to fetch the girls to see the display, this thought came back even more strongly to me.

"Your father," I told Ellen, "has no more imagination than a louse: Either that, or he is just too unfeeling himself to realise how grieved the Queen must be at the reason for all this."

"She does not know the reason." Ellen spoke in a very small voice that was quite unlike her usual confident tones. "He has not told her yet."

"Not told her!" I stared around the courtyard at the leaping flames of the fire, the fireworks spurting red and gold. "But why? He knows she can see it all from her window. And she has a *right* to be told the reason for it."

Ellen looked away without answering. I gripped her shoulder, and said angrily, "*You* could have told her. Why did you keep quiet?"

Ellen looked uncertainly at Margaret Lindsay, but Margaret was no help to her. "I – I wanted to speak," she faltered. "I said to Margaret that we should."

"Well?" I swung to face Margaret Lindsay. She startled away from me, and said defensively. "We had no orders. And do you think she would have believed, anyway, even if we had told her?"

"Why should she not? *You* heard it from Sir William. She would have had to believe you."

"I am getting tired of you, Will Douglas." Margaret stared at me, her face suddenly hostile. "You seem to think you know this Queen. But you do not. She was *born* a Queen. She has always lived as a Queen. She cannot conceive of herself as anything less. And can you not see what that means? She simply cannot believe – even now, in spite of all that has happened – she cannot make herself believe that the lords would really act on that Deed. And so what was the point of *us* trying to tell her that they have?"

Ellen spoke again, still in that small ashamed voice. "She has bidden us tell my father to come to her. She has jumped to the conclusion, you see, that all this must be for someone's birthday, and – " Ellen paused, seeming almost to choke on her words, and then rushed on to a finish. "You know how she loves birthday games, and how good she is at giving presents. She wants to join in the celebration."

I let them both go then, I was so sick at heart to hear all this. Yet still, when Sir William called me to him a few minutes later, there was no way to avoid his summons. I had to trot faithfully as always at his heels when he made his way up to the Queen's apartments; and, standing just inside the doorway there, I saw how she received him. She was smiling as she stood with one hand laid on the back of the chair beside her, the other hand fingering the gold crucifix that hung always around her neck; and when she spoke to him, her tone was light.

"Well, Sir William. You are all very merry tonight. But am I not to be allowed to join in the celebrations? It would please me, I must tell you, to add my share to the birthday scene."

And she would if she could, I thought despairingly. I still had the little gold comfit box she had given *me* on my tenth birthday. The taste of the sweets that had been in it filled my mouth suddenly again, as if I had just that moment eaten them, and my rage at Sir William was so strong that I wanted to strike him. And yet, I knew well, he was not a cruel man. For all my anger then, I knew it was not even true to call him an unfeeling one. It was simply a stupid man who stood there telling the Queen,

"But Your Grace, we have no birthday among us today. We are just celebrating the news."

"The news?"

"Why yes, Your Grace. The Deed you signed is law now. Your little son has been crowned King, and the Earl of Moray has been appointed Regent."

Now she *had* to believe! I thought she might collapse then, and anticipation of this made me feel sick again. But she took the blow without flinching, without even crying out. Her smile stiffened into a mask, then faded. The hand on the back of the chair tightened its grip. The fingers moving over the crucifix became still. And that was all. But not quite all, so far as Sir William was concerned!

He was waiting, still smiling with his own pleasure, for her to reply to his announcement. But it was no longer a lonely young woman, hungry for company, he had to deal with now. It was the Queen, with the full force of Royal dignity behind her continuing silence. I realised that as she gave an abrupt wave of dismissal, and then pointed this by turning haughtily from him.

He moved uncertainly to the door, looked at me as if asking what he had done to be treated so, then shrugged, and went out. I closed the door behind him. And no-one pays attention to a page. As I drew the door shut, the Queen sank to her knees beside her chair, and laid her head on her outstretched arms. I stood outside the door and listened; and the sound that came to me then was that of bitter, bitter sobbing.

I could not get that sound out of my mind. Especially at night, before I slept, it was with me. And two days later, when George returned to Lochleven, it was with me again as I told him of that night's events. George listened to me, his face tight with the same anger I had felt; but when I had finished, he sighed and said,

"But it is still not easy, Will, to kill hope – especially in someone who clings as strongly as she does to her hope of Moray. And she is now buoyed up in that, you see, by the mere fact of my bringing back word that Moray *will* come to visit her."

"But his own credit now demands he must do so," I argued. "Even I know that, George. And you must surely have tried to get her to see that too."

George sighed again. "Of course. I put it as strongly as I could to her."

"And if she finds that Moray will not do anything for her?"

"I talked with her on that as well," George said. "I told her how I used my time away from here to get in touch with some of those still faithful to her cause – "

"With the Earl Bothwell?" I could not help eagerly

interrupting then, it was so long since I had heard mention of Bothwell; but George shook his head to this.

"There can be no help from that quarter. Bothwell is now an outlaw, so ferociously pursued by Moray's forces that even the most loyal of the Queen's supporters dare not rally to him. And so I have informed her. Yet her spirit remains strong, in spite of that; and if Moray does indeed fail her, I have her permission to put my own plan of escape into practice."

I pushed the picture of the fugitive Bothwell to the back of my mind as it began to fill with visions of an assault force scaling the Castle walls; but George stopped me the moment I began to speak those new thoughts aloud.

"There will be no assault," he told me. "You know my brother. He would certainly think it proper to die in defence of his duty – and of his womenfolk, of course, because even they would be at risk in that kind of situation. And one thing I will *not* do is to put the lives of my family in danger."

"Then tell me what will happen," I begged. "And will I be allowed to take part in it?"

"Yes, I will need you," George admitted. "But as for the plan itself, I have already told you that the Queen's permission for that depends on whether or not Moray destroys the hope she rests on him. And so there is no point in speaking further of it until after he has been to see her."

I was tantalised out of my mind by this, but George was stubborn. I could not make him yield to tell me more; and so – like everyone else in the Castle after that – there was nothing I could do except to summon patience and wait for the promised day of Moray's visit to the Queen.

8

He was dressed all in black when he did appear, nearly two weeks from that time – no other point of colour about him except the silver that cased his sword, the silver buckles on his shoes, the white ruff around the neck of his black doublet.

Tall and thick-set, his dark hair and beard looking even darker against this one splash of white, he came treading slowly into the Great Hall. I was impressed, in spite of myself, at the air of sombre authority in his appearance; but every lion has its running-dog, I suppose, and so I was not surprised to see Lord Lindsay following first among those he had brought with him.

I noticed, also, that George was scowling at Lindsay's presence. Sir William did not look well pleased, either, at this. There was a low and hurried conversation between him and Moray; and the result, it seemed, was that Moray thought better of once more imposing Lindsay on the Queen. With a glance around his party, he beckoned the Earl of Morton to him, then the Earl of Athole; and it was these two, finally, who escorted him to the Queen's apartments.

We were a very subdued gathering once they had gone. Lindsay, and the rest of Moray's escort, stood apart from those in Sir William's household, their conversation held down to the lowest of whispers. Lindsay himself kept total silence; but even in silence his heavy features gave out menace, and this added to the uneasiness of that subdued atmosphere.

It was all setting Sir William very much on edge, I realised; and as the hour for supper drew near, he became quite markedly so. Would Moray sup with the Queen, he wondered; or with us? He was like a broody hen fussing over her nest, I told myself contemptuously. And then was suddenly ashamed of the thought.

Sir William, after all, had always been content to leave the politics of the Queen's situation to the Old Lady. Yet it was still he who carried the responsibility for her imprisonment; and so it was not a trifling point, this question of where Moray would sup that night. If he showed himself friendly enough to the Queen to sit at table with her, I realised, it could be a sign that she was managing to charm him into a promise of her freedom. And how then would Sir William be rewarded for his strictness to her?

The smell of hot food wafted suddenly into the Hall. I saw, beyond the service screen, the figure of the Provençal cook Diderot, holding a silver dish at arms' length before him. Some maids bearing other dishes clustered behind him, all of them waiting for Sir William to lead their suppertime procession up to the Queen's apartments. He went towards them, face creased with the worry of the moment. There was a further short wait while he tasted the food and the wine, then Diderot and the maids formed into procession to follow him upstairs.

The clattering of their feet on the stone steps echoed back to the Hall, faded, and died into nothing. For long moments of silence then, everyone in the Hall looked ceiling-wards, as if that could somehow give a view of what was happening in the apartments above. We heard a distant murmur of voices, as if the door to these apartments had been opened. One of the distant voices became suddenly clear, rising in pitch above the others; the Queen's voice crying out in protest,

'*My lord Moray! Brother! You used not to think it beneath you to give me the napkin at supper!*'

Moray had refused to sup with her. The silence in the Great Hall was rippled over with voices as this realisation came to everyone there. I looked towards Lindsay, and then towards George. Lindsay was grinning. George, when our eyes met, gave the smallest of shrugs; and plainer than words, it seemed to me, the gesture said,

"*Did I not tell you so!*"

The stairs echoed again to the tread of feet. Then Moray and the other two were once more among us, with Moray's cold gaze slowly taking in each face there before Sir William led him ceremoniously to the family supper-table.

I felt a twinge of fear at the renewed experience of that gaze. The warning Minny had once given me flashed back into my mind, and when I leaned over Moray's shoulder to pour his wine, my twinge became a fear so strong that I found myself breaking into a sweat. I must be mad, I thought, to make *this* man my enemy – because that was exactly what I would be doing if George's plan went forward, and if I took part in it. Nor would my lack of years save me if I were to be caught out in that – not from one so merciless as Moray!

I took the night to sleep on these fears, and the morning brought with it the reassurance that I could easily put distance between myself and Moray's vengeance. It was not so difficult, after all, to get a ship's passage to France; and many young Scotsmen had made good careers in that country. And there was England too, of course. Moray's writ did not run there either, and the thought of play-acting in London still attracted me.

I went straight in search of George, once Moray and his retinue had departed, and found him checking weapons in the barracks armoury. I made sure there was no-one else within earshot, then quickly challenged,

"The plan, George – does it go on?"

George nodded. "More than ever now. There is no hope of Moray ever arranging the Queen's release. He made that crystal clear to her last night; and again to Sir William and myself before he left this morning. And so listen carefully, Will." He paused to check, as I had done, against being overheard. "We are going to take the Castle *from the inside*, with the help of Captain Drysdale, and another eight men of the Guard. I have sounded out all of these, and all are willing."

"And my part in this?" I spoke so eagerly that George smiled as he told me,

"Your part will be the next step in the arrangements I have already made. The members of the force I have gathered are all discreetly quartered on the mainland, and I want you to take a boat over there now. At the Kinross Inn, then, you will seek out a gentleman by the name of John Beaton; and you will give this message from me. *The barge is ready for loading.*"

"The barge is ready –" I checked myself there. "Do you mean *our* barge? The one we send every week to the mainland for our supplies?"

George nodded. "The very same. Beaton and his men will seize it when it touches tomorrow as usual, at the mainland landing-stage. When I see them bringing it back here I will give the order to make prisoners of the Queen's guards, and to overpower Sir William – but without hurting him, of course. The rest of the Guard will then be leaderless, we will have Beaton's force to assist us – not to mention the joint authority of Captain Drysdale and myself; and so, in the end, they are not likely to offer much resistance."

I did not wait to press George for any elaboration of this; nor did he need to tell me anything further of my part. George knew as well as I did that too long an absence from my usual duties would earn me a beating from Sir William. And he was well aware also of my method of slipping away from the island with the least risk of being noticed.

I ran straight for our east landing-stage – the one we used when a wind from the west made the loch too rough to beach our boats at the more convenient stage facing west to the mainland. The east stage was where I always kept my own little boat. I set my usual course in this, and twelve minutes after speaking to George I was tying up at the public landing-stage for the ferry-boats plying out of Kinross. To my right then, I could see the pepper-pot shape of the roof on the tower that buttressed the Kinross Inn; and another minute or so later, I was strolling casually into the Inn's taproom.

There were only a few people there. I noted Jock Matheson, the innkeeper, the fat and talkative woman who was Mistress Matheson, two men playing dice with another man watching them, a group of four men sipping slow and silent at their ale, and one man sitting alone over a glass of wine. The solitary man was dressed like a gentleman, while the others were clearly not of that standing. I studied him covertly while Matheson drew the ale I ordered, and decided to take a chance on this being the mysterious John Beaton.

There was an empty stool beside the one he occupied. I sauntered towards it, and politely asked, "Sir, if I may share your corner – ?"

His glance at me, I thought, was sharper than any gentleman had a right to give a stranger. On the other hand, if he was expecting a messenger such as myself... Without any answer except a wave and a nod, he granted my request. I set my ale on the trestle in front of the stool, seated myself, and spoke low to him.

"I thank you, Mr – er – Beaton, is it not?"

This time there was no doubt of the sharpness in his glance at me, nor of the sudden wariness in his long, thin features. "Who told *you* my name is Beaton? Who are you?"

"I am Will Douglas, from Lochleven." I sipped my ale, counselling myself to go a little more carefully now. "And if you will tell me *your* full name, sir, I may find you are indeed the same Mr Beaton who should have the message I carry."

"Go on drinking your ale," he told me, "and talk about sport, the weather – anything – before you say more on that score."

I drank my ale; and, quiet as ever, he continued, "My full name is John Beaton. I am brother to Archbishop Beaton, the Queen's Ambassador to France. And the message *I* expect is from Mr George Douglas."

I talked about the good sport there was in flying hawks from Lochleven, about fishing for trout in the loch, about the miserably wet summer we were having. Then at last I slipped into our conversation George's message – "*The barge is ready for loading.*" Our murmuring voices went on from there.

"*And the day?*"

"*Tomorrow.*"

"*The time?*"

"*It touches the mainland at nine o'clock in the morning.*"

"*All other procedures will be as agreed?*"

"*That is what I have been told.*"

"*Then you may let Mr Douglas know he need not fear for my share.*"

John Beaton rose with leisurely ease. His voice louder now, he spoke in the same vein he had earlier advised for me. "Well, my lad, I am much obliged to know the fishing is so good this year. But I have a few matters calling my attention now; and so . . ."

With a brief bow to myself, a nod and a pleasant "Good-day" all around, he was gone. I spun out the business of finishing my ale so as to give myself a decent interval before following his example; and by the time I left the Inn I was fairly hugging myself over the success of my mission.

The elation that bore me up then persisted long after I had got back to the Castle, long after I had given Beaton's message to George. And lying awake that night with my mind painting bright pictures on

75

darkness, I rehearsed my own possible share in the next day's rescue scene. I would be on hand, I vowed, when George went with the soldiers to over-power the guards on the Queen's door. Not that I had ever used a sword before, of course, except in fencing lessons; but given the chance, I still saw no reason why I should not be able to put in at least a few bold and useful strokes.

I slept uneasily that night, perhaps because of my excitement, and in the dreams that plagued my sleep it seemed to me I could hear faintly the sound of hammers striking on metal. I woke to an odd sense of foreboding I could not name until memory of the previous day came rushing back; and the one thing I wanted to do then was to watch the barge being pushed out for its trip to the mainland.

As soon as I could after Sir William had unlocked the gate in the courtyard wall, I ran down to the west landing-stage. The usual mooring place for the barge was empty – and yet it was still only eight o'clock in the morning, which meant I could not possibly have been too late to see it go out. I looked hurriedly right and left. And then I saw it – dragged right up on land, and chained with thick steel chains to the outer wall of the Castle.

The dream-sound of hammers striking on metal came rushing back to me; and this time, I knew, I had not dreamed it. More than that, I realised, the barge was not intended to sail that day – or any other day, for that matter of it. There was no way of slipping those chains free. They were, as they had been intended to be, a fixture.

"A good piece of work, eh?"

The question sounding sudden and harsh at my elbow startled me out of my trance of dismay. I turned swiftly to see Captain Drysdale looming over me – Drysdale, who was to have been our accomplice, and who now sounded so complacent over the ruin of our plan! Years of dislike for the man's surly nature gathered instantly to back up the suspicion in my mind. Warily, I said,

"It was Sir William ordered it done, I suppose."

"Who else?" Drysdale grinned, the thin-lipped grin that always made him look like a fox, and smugly added, "But on my advice, of course."

I wanted desperately to ask why he had been so treacherous, but could not, for fear of letting him know my own involvement. And what about George? Did he know yet that his plan had been foiled? I made an excuse to leave Drysdale and hurried back through the courtyard gate. But it was another hour after that – well after the barge's usual departure time – before I could find George; and one look exchanged between us then was enough to make each of us aware that the other knew what had happened.

" I have warned Beaton," George said quietly. "I rowed out as soon as I saw the barge had been chained."

"And you know that we have Drysdale to blame?"

"I know. And I was a fool to trust him. There is no need," George assured me grimly, "to rub salt into *that* wound."

I bit back the reproach I had been about to make, and asked instead, "But why? Why did Drysdale pretend to be with you and then go straight to betray the plan to Sir William?"

"Because –" George hesitated, and then said all in a rush, "Because he thinks the same of the Queen as Lindsay does. He believes all the vile stories about her. And so he hates her. As do the two men he has put on guard at her door. He chose them specially for that reason – which is something else we have to put to our account with him."

George was flushed by then, and almost inarticulate with anger. I waited for him to calm down; and, more quietly at last, he added, "Or so I learned, at least, from my brother when he challenged me about the barge."

I gasped in dismay. I had forgotten George would have to reckon with Sir William's anger over the escape attempt! Hurriedly I asked,

"But what did he say about you? Will you be banished the Castle?"

George shook his head. "That would be as good – or as bad – as admitting that Lochleven is not so secure as my brother ought to have made it, and thus to draw the lords' censure down on his own head. I am to be barred from the Queen's presence, that is all – for the time being, at least."

"And so what do we do now?"

"I try, if I can, to discover the Queen's wishes before we decide on that. But as for how I am to do so . . ."

George paused, frowning over the question this posed. But *I* had the answer to it, all ready on the tip of my tongue. Arnault! Fat, cunning, and "blindly-loyal" M'sieur Arnault had daily access to the Queen; and where could we find a better go-between than that little man?

9

"Give her time," was Arnault's first advice. "Her Grace is still melancholy over her failure with Moray – too much so to be ready yet for active planning."

We bore patiently for a week, and by the end of that time Arnault was reporting back to us.

"Her Grace is utterly determined on one thing, Messieurs. She will not let her cause go by default. She will not cease, therefore, to demand both her freedom and the right to appear before the lords to defend her name. She enquires, therefore, M'sieu Douglas, if you are still willing to be her messenger to the Earl of Moray."

"If that is her wish," George agreed. "But what of escape, M'sieu Arnault. Has she spoken any further of that?"

Arnault was enjoying his role of intermediary, it seemed to me. His tone became measured and rather pompous as he told us then,

"Indeed she has. But she is now convinced that escape in itself is not enough. It will be of no use to her, in fact, to take advantage of any plan to free her until she first knows she can rely on having an army strong enough to defeat the one that Moray is certain to bring against her. To that end, therefore, she wishes to establish a courier service, with myself to smuggle out the letters she writes, and with you to carry them ashore to M'sieur John Beaton – who will then pass them further along the chain."

George said thoughtfully, "That makes sense, I agree. But M'sieu Arnault – "

Arnault checked him with one pudgy hand upheld. "And since the Queen's supporters in Scotland are in such disarray," he continued, "she intends to write also to France, to her kinfolk there, asking them to supply troops to back up her Scottish force, and thus be sure of final victory."

"But all that will take weeks to arrange," George exclaimed. "Months, perhaps, if the French are slow in their agreement. And time is short. Winter will soon be on us; and you know that armies can neither march nor invade in winter weather."

"You asked to know Her Grace's mind," Arnault pointed out. "And I have spoken it, exactly as she instructed me."

"I realise that." George was looking agitated now. "But delay could be dangerous for her. I have told you already how dangerous it could be."

"But she does not accept that," Arnault retorted. "And I am not the one to bring it home to her. What is more, I doubt if anyone could – yourself included. Her faith in her own innocence of any crime, M'sieu, is too strong for that."

Neither of them had been paying the least attention to me in the course of all this. Nor could I make head or tail of that remark about the Queen's "innocence"; and when George gave no answer to it, I grew impatient.

"Writing materials," I reminded the other two. "If

the Queen is to have a courier service, she must first have pens, ink, and paper.''

Arnault raised a grin for my benefit. "You have such common-sense," he told me, "that I could almost believe you have French blood in you."

I glanced aside at George and said, "All I know of my blood is the name I bear." This was enough to raise some sort of grin from him too; and after that, we turned to the practical side of arranging the courier service.

Paper was the real problem; because paper, of course, was far too precious to be easily available. But Arnault had a small stock that was enough to begin with, and when this ran out, I robbed Sir William's desk for more. Until, that is, I discovered Lady Agnes at the same game; and since Lady Agnes knew I was well aware she had never been able to write more than her own name, she was immediately startled into confessing the reason for her theft.

"'Tis for a – a journal. A private journal the Queen wishes to keep of her days here," she stuttered, and peered over the desk at me with big, cow-like eyes nervously blinking. "But you are not to tell, Will, because you know Sir William has ordered she is not to have any writing materials. And you would not want to get both Her Grace and me into trouble, would you?"

I promised faithfully I would not tell; and gave silent thanks, meanwhile, to the providence that had made Lady Agnes so stupid, as well as so kind-hearted. I also took great care, thereafter, to shuffle around the contents of Sir William's desk so that he would not notice when Lady Agnes thieved paper from it. But that was tame work. And it was always George, of course, who took the Queen's letters to the mainland.

I longed for diversion – any kind of diversion to while away the waiting time; and so I took to gambling again, with some of the Castle Guard for my opponents and another of my silver buttons for a stake.

"But this is the last time," Minny warned as she sewed a replacement on for me. "I'll not protect your hide again from the Old Lady, if you lose this one like you lost the other."

Minny always meant what she said; and so, after I had won enough to buy back my first button and have a little money over, I bowed out of the game. That was when I started slipping across to the mainland to see a girl I knew there – the daughter of the fat and talkative Mistress Matheson, who was landlady of the Kinross Inn. Muriel, they called this daughter. She was slender, with dark hair, and dark eyes that sent out signals telling me I could make progress with her. But the fat mother was watching us too closely for that; and so my chance of diversion at the Inn also came to nothing.

"I envy you," I told George. I had glimpsed him now and then at the Inn talking low and earnestly to John Beaton, and others who were strangers to me. But George's eyes had avoided mine on these occasions; and now he told me,

"The less you know at this point, my lad, the better for all of us."

"Why?" I was feeling resentful by then, and the sharpness of George's answer showed how well he realised this.

"Because ignorance will be your only shield, of

course, if anyone questions you about me."

I tried another tack. "Have you thought any more about escape, George? Because we should be ready with some kind of plan, should we not? Even if the Queen herself wants to delay the matter."

"I have thought – of course I have," George admitted. "But every possibility that comes to me finishes up by seeming wilder than the one before."

"To take the Castle by storm –" I began; but fiercely George cut across me.

"I told you my reasons against that! And I have made those clear too, to Beaton and the others. I will *not* risk the lives of my family."

I shrugged, and gave in. Our talk began to centre on other prospects for escape, but always we came up against the same obstacles. Even if we could get the Queen past the guard on her door, the gate in the courtyard wall was still the only exit from the Castle. By day, also, when the gate stood open, there were soldiers on guard there too. At night, at seven o'clock precisely, Sir William locked the gate. And the key to the gate was never out of his possession.

"But we must keep worrying at the problem," George insisted. "Because I *will* be banished from Lochleven if I am discovered to be still active on her behalf. And that will leave only you to keep in touch with me then; you, and only you, to carry out any possible rescue plan."

I liked the sound of that! Not because I wished George any harm, of course; but the prospect of rescuing the Queen entirely on my own *was* an attractive one. "I will keep on thinking," I assured him. "And if we can find a plan and you are banished, I promise I will carry it out as faithfully as you would yourself."

The glow of my conversation with George did not last. It was still only a far-off possibility, after all, this prospect he had held out; and the immediate prospect was only that of yet another dull winter in Lochleven. My envy began to stretch to cover the situation of Ellen and Margaret, so well-placed to enjoy themselves now that the Queen had recovered from her fit of melancholy. And I was not alone in this.

The Queen still wept sometimes in the night, the girls said, and she prayed as much as she had always done. But even so, she was making good use now of the lute, the cards, the chessmen, and all the various other things she had asked for to lighten the burden of her imprisonment; and every day in her apartments now, there was music, and singing, games of skill and chance, lively conversation, and romps that were even livelier.

"And dancing," Ellen reported enthusiastically. "Margaret and I have learned some beautiful dances from her."

"Have you indeed!" Sir William exclaimed; and the slight edge of his voice reminded me that Ellen was the favourite among his children, the only one he had not been content to leave under the Old Lady's care in the New House. Sir William, I thought, was missing the company he was accustomed to have from Ellen; and when I went with him each day on his official visits to the Queen, it seemed to me that these visits were becoming longer.

"I must say," he told the Old Lady, "that Her Grace seems to have become most resigned to her situation."

The Old Lady shrugged. "Her religion is a

comfort to her, I suppose. And she does have a sweetness of nature which could also account for that. Besides, her wings have been well and truly clipped, now that the matter of the Regency has been so firmly settled."

"Then why should we not be more friendly to her?" Lady Agnes asked. "*I* find it pleasant enough to spend the day sitting with her."

The Old Lady gave Lady Agnes a glance that said, *"You would!"* But Lady Agnes was at the start of yet another addition to her family, and was far too content with herself to notice this. "The Queen," she went on, "is making such a beautiful tapestry, it is a joy to behold. And there always seems to be so much to talk about, too, with her and her ladies."

That drew the Old Lady! She could never bear to be left out of anything; and quite apart from that, she still craved the kind of Court gossip she had enjoyed in her youth. The Old Lady also began to visit the Queen's apartments; and sharp as her tongue was, it could also be a very amusing one. The length of Sir William's own visits increased when he found both her and Lady Agnes in the Queen's apartments. The visits themselves became less and less official, the traffic in and out of the Queen's apartments more and more casual; until finally, out of all this, it began to seem the most natural thing in the world for the whole family to be gathered there for at least some time each day. And if the rest of us could be there, then why not George also?

Casually one day, the Queen put this question to the Old Lady. There was no-one, after all, who had a neater foot in the dance than young Mr Douglas – or so *she* had been told, at least. And so it was a pity, was it not, that her ladies were being deprived of the opportunity to admire his skill?

Little Jane Kennedy and tall Maria de Courcelles looked modestly downwards. The Queen smiled, and teasingly reminded them how handsome Mr Douglas was. Oh yes, Kennedy agreed demurely, she had noticed that. de Courcelles lifted her own very handsome head to acknowledge it would indeed be so much more pleasant to have the company of young Mr Douglas also.

I watched the faces of Sir William and the Old Lady as they talked. Sir William had the air of a man who pretends not to hear the conversation around him, but the Old Lady was fairly preening with pleasure in all this talk about George. *"Pretty Geordie"* – it was she, I remembered, who had so fondly invented that nickname for him; and as my eyes came to rest on her then I wondered how I could have been so blind to the strategy of all the seemingly-harmless diversions that had brought us to this moment.

"You could have told me," I reproached George, "instead of leaving me to guess."

The arguments bred from that conversation about him were over by then. Sir William had finally agreed with the Old Lady that George had learned his lesson; and now George had the same freedom of the Queen's apartments as the rest of us had. He grinned, to begin with, at the peevish tone of my voice, and teased me,

"But maybe you are not so good an actor as you think you are!"

"And what has that to do with it?"

"A great deal, my lad. The Queen was well aware I

would never be allowed into her presence until she had disarmed all suspicion of herself. And if there had been one unguarded look or word from you, my brother might just have guessed where all her entertainments were leading him."

"I would still have preferred the chance to act the fool," I retorted, "rather than to know you have made one of me."

"Oh come," George coaxed. "Think of what has been accomplished. There is no longer any need for Arnault to act as go-between. And supposing there should be a situation where I have to see the Queen alone. Her guards will let me pass without question now. And is all that not worth a little sacrifice of pride on your part?"

I could not think of any argument to this; and so went sulkily off instead to the game of cards the Queen had commanded I should play with her. She was a worthy opponent, I had discovered; but she had a gambling streak that ran as deep and wide as my own, and I happened that day to be holding the better cards. At the end of the game, she paid up handsomely; and I was not only feeling in better mood by then, but in better shape also to play this other game she had so skilfully devised for us.

"I told you – remember?" Ellen challenged me. I said it could be exciting for all of us to have her here. And it *is* now. You have to admit that, Will. We are like people at Court now, are we not? And all of us really enjoying ourselves!"

"*All* of us?"

The smile Ellen had turned on me began to falter. "I know what you mean by that, Will Douglas; but you are wrong. Margaret does not laugh and sing the way I do because it is her nature to be quiet. And *she* cannot help the way her father behaved to the Queen."

"You spoke of disarming suspicion," I told George, "but I do not think we can yet be certain of Margaret Lindsay where that is concerned."

Jane Kennedy took up the lute for one of the galliards she played so well, and it was George who won the Queen's hand for the dance. The eyes of the Old Lady and Lady Agnes followed its movement, and Lady Agnes said wistfully,

"I wish I could dance like that."

The Old Lady glanced from the light, floating form of the Queen to the plump one of Lady Agnes; and with bright eyes sparking malice, she asked, "How could you when you do not look like that, even when you are not with child?"

I caught Ellen's eye and grinned to see her so embarrassed at this. The Old Lady and Lady Agnes went on bickering. Ellen moved to give me a pinch in the ribs for my impudence. Under cover of the music we started our own argument, then were silent again as Kennedy stopped playing, and George led the Queen back to her chair.

"But of course, Your Grace," he was telling her, "my sisters would be deeply honoured to meet you."

The Queen leaned forward in smiling anticipation as he turned to announce to the rest of us, "Her Grace has expressed a desire to meet the Seven Lochleven Porches. And she is curious to know why they are called so."

We glanced from one to the other, smiling at this,

before the Old Lady said, "When you meet my daughters, Your Grace, you will understand. They look like their nickname – all of them as tall, and slender, and straight as the pillars of a porch."

"And swan-necked too," George added, "which gives a beautiful curve to the summit of each Porch!"

Our smiles broke into laughter then, but hard on this laughter came a voice, the small and clear voice of Margaret Lindsay saying,

"But Your Grace, my mother is one of them. And surely you cannot wish to meet now with *her*."

Embarrassed silence gripped the room. But the Queen's smile did not falter, and when she spoke, her voice was gentle. "Why not, child? Lady Lindsay has not harmed me, any more than you have."

A flush leapt into Margaret's sallow face. Impulsively she knelt to kiss the Queen's hand. And it was Margaret herself, the next day, who shyly led her mother as the first of the Seven Lochleven Porches to make their curtsies to the Queen.

Genteelly then, they sipped the wine I poured for them, congratulated Lady Agnes on her condition, clustered around to hear the Queen explain the intricate pattern of her tapestry work. They scolded me, too, for having spent so long without visiting them. I teased them in reply, for taking so long over finding husbands for themselves; and thought how right Ellen had been. It really was most pleasant, this little Court the Queen had created around her own presence.

I looked again towards where she sat in a high-backed chair, with Sir William and George and the Porches gathered about her, Ellen and Margaret crouched at her feet. The polished wood of the chair made a dark frame for her head and face. The red-gold of her hair, the paleness of her skin, glowed from the frame with their own soft and mysterious light that moved as she moved when she glanced from one to the other of the surrounding group. And they were all so fascinated by her!

This little Court, I thought, was a sort of dream she had spun for them, with herself as the bright centre that drew their eyes inward from the world beyond the walls of Lochleven – the real world of power and war over kingdoms. And – except for George – not one of them could see how skilfully she was charming their attention away from her purpose of re-entering that real world.

Sir William, I noticed, was bending a little, the better to hear her speaking. Ellen and Margaret were looking up into her face, and Margaret's eyes were as adoring now as those of Ellen. The Porches were all listening intently to her, and all standing very deferentially in the correct Court positions. She began speaking directly to the seven of them, telling them first that she had been accustomed always to walk or ride for some part of every day, and then wistfully confessing how much and how often this made her long to be allowed again into the fresh air of the garden.

And there was Sir William now, flinching back from the accusation in seven sisterly pairs of eyes, the reproach in seven sisterly voices! There was Sir William being forced to agree,

"Why yes, if the day is good enough, Her Grace may take a turn in the garden. I should be pleased to escort her."

So he was taking no risks there, even although he had been cornered into this further permission. But he had at least granted it. And it did at least mean that the Queen could now be seen leaving her apartments without an instant alarm being raised. One more small victory, I thought, for the Court of Dreams!

The Lochleven Porches departed, there was space again for dancing; and when Kennedy struck a chord on the lute, Sir William bowed Maria de Courcelles to the floor. She was nearly as tall as he was, and the glossiness of her dark hair looked well against his ruddy fairness. But Sir William's features were coarsened with middle age. Moreover, he was nowhere near so slim as George, who had now taken the Queen on his arm; and so it was George and the Queen who made by far the better couple. The Old Lady called Ellen to her, and said,

"You see there, Ellen, how tall the Queen is. And yet George is an even height with her. Now let that be a lesson to you because you are going to be tall, like your aunts, the Porches. And half the reason that six of *them* are still unmarried is that they make themselves look ridiculous by consenting to dance with men who are not even their equals in height."

Ellen bent to whisper something to the Old Lady. I thought, from their faces, it might be a question. The Old Lady drew back from Ellen and looked towards George and the Queen. I looked also, and found I could not take my eyes from them.

The Queen was dancing with her head back-tilted, so that her smile at George seemed to slant a little. The amber gleam of her eyes reflected her smile. The light in the room made a glisten on the delicate skin of her throat, like the glisten of the pearls fringing the white of the heart-shaped coif on her hair. And George was gazing at all this with so deep a longing in his eyes that there was no mistaking the fact. *George was in love with her!*

It was the sound of the Old Lady calling me to bring her a footstool that startled me back to the rest of the room. I hurried to obey the call; and as I knelt to lift her feet on to the stool, she said softly,

"You are not to get mixed up in any plans that George may have. D'ye hear me?"

I was too surprised to make an instant recovery from the effect of this. I tried to rise, mumbling some sort of denial of any intent whatsoever, and found myself pinned there by one bony hand pressing into my shoulder. Under her breath, the Old Lady hissed at me,

"Stop lying, Will. I always know when you are lying. You were very thick with George for a while back there. But you will let him take his own risks from now on, or answer to me for it."

I nodded, not daring to trust my voice; and she released me, to sit back and resume her watch on the dancers. To my further surprise then, I saw that her gaze at George and the Queen had an air of grim satisfaction about it – like that of an old tigress, I thought, watching her cub at play!

I rose towards the tray of wine, and while I pretended to put the cups on it in order, I tried to bring some order also into my thoughts on the scene that had just taken place. But there was one thing about it that defeated me. I simply could not see why the Old Lady – of all people – should seem pleased that George was in love with the Queen. And, I realised, I would never keep abreast of events now until I had the answer to *that* riddle!

10

Minny went off at a tangent with *her* answer.

" 'Tis not easy," she said wistfully, "being in love. It can be a sore thing, Will. A very sore thing."

Harking back to her own young days, I thought, and turned swiftly from the uncomfortable feeling that Minny's sore experience of love might have been the reason for my own existence.

"That was not my point, Minny," I reminded. "It was the Old Lady I asked about – why she should be so content to see George in love with the Queen."

Minny stared blankly at me. "Why should she not? Mr George is handsome. His blood is most noble, and he is of an age to give the Queen many children. It would be a good match – and the Old Lady would certainly delight to see a King's crown on the head of her pretty Geordie!"

"But Minny, the Queen is already married. To Bothwell."

Minny's stare became one of pity. "You *are* green, Will," she told me. "Forget Bothwell. He is a fugitive now. An exile in Norway, they say. The Queen could get a divorce from him for any one of half a dozen reasons. Or else she could have the marriage to him annulled. And the Old Lady knows that as well as I do."

"But even so," I protested, "you are going too fast. The Queen cannot make a King of George until she has won back her throne. And she cannot do that until she has got out of here and fought a battle with Moray. But even if she does succeed in all these things, and even if she owes her success to George's help, it does not mean to say she would marry him."

"No," Minny admitted. "But the chance is there, is it not? And trust the Old Lady to be wide-awake to that!"

"And Moray?" I demanded. "What about him and her pride in him as Regent? There would be no more power for Moray if the Queen were to win back her Throne."

"Of course," Minny agreed. "But to have George for King would give the Old Lady even more cause for pride, would it not? And besides, laddie, she knows very well there is nothing she can do now to stop him in his tracks – not if he is as much in love with the Queen as you say he is."

"She could warn Moray."

"No, no." Decisively Minny shook her head. "She might be content for Mr George to 'take his own risks', as you called it. But he is still her youngest, her precious ewe-lamb. And so *she'll* not be the one to put his very life at stake."

Suddenly then, I remembered what the Old Lady herself had said, months before, when she had insisted on Arnault being brought to treat the Queen's illness. *"I have more sons than Moray."* Minny was right, I realised. The Old Lady would indeed let matters take their course now. And if Moray *was* destined to be toppled eventually from his high position as Regent, why should she not console herself with the hope of George being raised even higher?

But supposing the Queen did not want to divorce Bothwell – or to have her marriage to him annulled? I would need someone other than Minny to answer that for me, I decided. Minny was shrewd enough in reading the Old Lady's mind; but the someone I needed now would have to be equally shrewd in reading the mind of the Queen!

Arnault, at first, was very decisive. "You can be certain of one thing," he told me. "As a faithful daughter of the Roman Church, the Queen would never consider divorce."

"And annulment?"

"Well, yes," he allowed. "She might agree to that – but only if she saw a need for it."

"A political need – is that what you mean?"

"Precisely. But why do you ask all this?"

"Because George is in love with the Queen. And the Old Lady thinks she might marry him."

To my surprise then, Arnault chuckled and said, "I knew that would happen. I knew it!"

"Oh, so you knew, did you?" I challenged. "Because that was also part of the Queen's strategy?"

"Not at all, my young friend." Arnault continued to grin at me. "But what happens when you put a honey-pot down among bees? They swarm towards it, they cannot resist its attractions. And that is the measure of Her Grace's charm. That is how she has succeeded in drawing you all into this – what did you call it? – this Court of Dreams. As for young M'sieur Douglas, has she shown him any more favour there than she has to the rest of you?"

I thought back to the moment I had realised George was drowning deep in love with the Queen, and compared her expression then with the inviting looks sent out by the inn-keeper's blackeyed daughter. "No" I admitted. "She has never played the coquette, or given him any sign of love. And would she mary him, M'sieu Arnault, without love?"

Arnault's grin turned sour at this; and grimly, he said, "She did without love in her marriage to Bothwell."

"But why?" I was asking this, I realised, with all sorts of confused thoughts about the Queen rushing suddenly into my mind. Arnault must have sensed this, because he answered me with a question of his own. "Why do *you* think she married him?"

The memories lurking behind my thoughts began to surface – Lord Lindsay shóuting "*Slut*" and "*Whore*" at the Queen, myself and Ellen quarrelling over the way Ellen had parrotted Lindsay's opinions of her character. "How can I tell," I hedged, "when all I know is what people say of her?"

"And people say she is a light woman, a wanton!" Arnault spoke angrily now, his dark face beginning to flush. "They say that Bothwell was her lover, even before Darnley was murdered. And do you know how much truth there is in that?"

I shook my head. "I told you. All I do know is rumour."

"But now you are troubled for young M'sieur Douglas," Arnault jeered. "And so now also, you will let rumour condemn her."

I looked at him then in even greater confusion. Those memories and the pictures that had surfaced along with them were so much at variance with my recent recollections of a Queen who could be one moment a laughing girl, and the next, a mysterious presence of majesty – or a kindly young woman teaching the steps of a dance; the Queen who was high-spirited, yet always repelled by anything gross or coarse, who wept in the night, and spent long hours in private prayer... Awkwardly I told Arnault.

"You do me wrong, M'sieu. It is just that – well, I do not believe the rumours about her, and I do not want to believe them. But I would like to understand."

"Understand what?" Arnault looked with hostility at me. "The truth? Because that was what I offered you."

I nodded, too over-awed by his expression to do more. Arnault gave a grunt of grim satisfaction. "Then let me instruct you a little," he said. "There are certain matters a woman cannot hide from her physician, any more that she can hide these matters from her confessor. It is therefore as Her Majesty's physician I speak when I say that the stories you have heard of her affair with Bothwell are false – all false."

He was glaring at me, daring me to speak further. I took my courage in both hands, and told him, "I need to hear more than that, M'sieu Arnault, if I am truly to understand. Because she did marry Bothwell after Darnley was murdered. Only a little more than three months afterwards! And everyone says it was Bothwell who did the murder."

"And for once," Arnault jeered, "everyone is right! Which proves?"

I almost failed then, before the sardonic note in his voice; but having come thus far, I had to nerve myself to go on. "I do not know what it proves," I told him. "But people also say it was she who incited

Bothwell to the murder. And to buy his silence over it, she had to marry him."

"Then people lie! Once again I tell you they lie, they lie!" Arnault was exclaiming loudly now, the flush on his face growing deeper with every word. "It was not till the day *after* the Queen married Bothwell that she knew he was the murderer. And if you do not believe me on that, ask the Spanish Ambassador to her Court. The English Ambassador too. *They* heard her calling in anguish for a knife to kill herself!"

Arnault was shaking with anger by this time. I shrank from him, hardly able to believe that a man of his sardonic humour should also have in him so much of passion. "But believe me you shall," he was finally insisting, "for the very good reason that I was there when she seized the knife; and it was I – Arnault – who wrenched it from her hand."

I gave the little man a moment to calm himself; and then, as quietly as I could, I told him, "You are so sure of your facts, M'sieu Arnault, that I must believe you. But none of this answers the very first question I asked, because I still do not know why the Queen should have chosen to marry Bothwell."

Arnault said wearily, "He had one great virtue in her eyes. She was surrounded by treacherous, self-seeking men, but he had always been utterly loyal to her. She knew she could count on him to support her in the terrible confusion following on Darnley's murder. And you have seen Bothwell in her retinue in the days when she used to visit this place. You must know the nature of the man."

Did I? I recalled Bothwell as I had seen him in the Queen's entourage – a fiercely-energetic man, swarthy, almost ugly, yet with something compelling in the glitter of his dark eyes ...

"Ambitious," Arnault said, "a clever soldier, and a man who knows only one way with women – the Queen included. Shrewd enough too, to make sure the chance of marriage to her did not slip by him then. And so he simply arranged matters so that she would have no honourable course except to marry him. He took her by force. And that, my young friend, was the extent of the 'choice' she had."

I said nothing to this. I was too appalled then to speak. Arnault was silent for a while also, his gaze far away and mournful; but finally he roused himself enough to say, "It is the tragedy of this poor young Queen, you see, that she has always needed to lean on someone stronger than herself. And for the short time that mattered, alas, it was her mistake to lean on Bothwell."

"She is leaning on no-one now!" I said this impulsively, and was surprised myself at the force of conviction behind it. "It was not George who planned her courier service or the way she has disarmed suspicion of herself. Nor was it you, M'sieu Arnault."

Arnault rubbed thoughtfully at the stubble that passed, with him, for a beard. "True," he agreed. "And it is also true there have been other times when she has surprised everyone by acting for herself – with skill too, and great courage. But that was always in situations she could defeat with one bold stroke; and this present one is different from those others. This one has forced her into a waiting game, just when delay spells danger to her. And so, you see, all the strength she has brought to it could count for nothing in the end."

That made twice I had heard this mysterious reference to "delay" and "danger". I would not let it pass this time, I decided; and bluntly I told Arnault, "No, I do not see. And I have been kept long enough in the dark over it. I think it is high time you told me, M'sieu Arnault, what *is* this danger you speak of?"

Arnault did not answer straightaway. Instead, he turned from me to sit at his desk, elbows propped, chin resting on clasped hands. From this position he gave me a long considering look, and only then did he say,

"It is not I who should rattle the skeleton in the Douglas family cupboard. Ask your friend – your blood relative M'sieu Georges, and see if *he* is willing to tell you."

I waited by the west landing-stage when I knew George had a letter to take to the mainland, making my duty of looking after the Castle boats an excuse to linger there. It was a cold day, real November weather, with sleet in the wind driving over the loch. George came hurrying down to the boats with the fur collar of his cloak pulled well up around his ears; and immediately I tackled him,

"I have been speaking to Arnault, George."

"And – ?" George was so impatient to be off he was barely listening.

"He told me about the Queen and Bothwell – the truth about the marriage between them."

That startled him into attention. He shot me a puzzled look, and asked, "Why did you want to know?"

What would he say, I wondered, if I told him the real reason? I decided to hedge, and said defensively, "Why should I not, when I find her so different from the picture that rumour has painted of her?"

George began to smile a little. "Good lad," he said softly. "I always knew you were a good lad behind that careless face you wear."

That was the conversation finished so far as he was concerned, but I caught his arm as he slipped the mooring-rope of the boat, and urgently told him,

"There was something else, George. Arnault spoke of the Queen playing a waiting game, and the danger this could be to her – just as you did once. But when I asked him what the danger was, he would not tell me. He said I must ask you."

George looked sharply at me. "Was that all he said?"

"No. He said –" I hesitated, and then awkwardly quoted, "*It is not I who should rattle the skeleton in the Douglas family cupboard.*"

"Arnault," said George grimly, "has quite a sense of humour!" He gave a savage little jerk of the mooring-rope, and then asked, "What else did he tell you?"

"About Darnley's murder. He said it was true that Bothwell did it, but that the Queen did not know that till after she married him."

"Exactly!" George exclaimed. "And so the skeleton, you see, is beginning to rattle!"

I had my own share of the Douglas temper, and that was when I felt it beginning to rise. I said, "Look, George, you said the day might come when I would have to act alone for the Queen. That means I will be running the same risks as you do now – perhaps more, because you are Moray's half-brother, and I am not. And so I think it only fair that you stop being so mysterious with me."

George nodded. "Yes. You are right. But 'tis the mere fact of being Moray's half-brother that makes it difficult to tell you. Because he has always been good to me, Will. More than good . . ."

I swallowed my rising anger and waited while George looked out into the driving sleet.

"Bothwell killed Darnley," he said at last; "but Bothwell was only the catspaw in that. There were others who wanted Darnley dead. They encouraged him to the murder; and the bait they held out was that – once the deed was done – they would support his ambition to marry the Queen."

"Others?"

"Men of Moray's party. The very ones who made the marriage an excuse to raise rebellion against her."

"But George –!" I caught George's arm and shook it in an attempt to make him face me. "Moray was not even in the country when the lords rebelled. You know that! He was in France."

"Of course." Now George did turn, of his own accord, his face pinched by the cold and working with an emotion I could only guess at. "Moray always has excelled at making bullets for others to fire!"

I dropped my hold on George's arm and took a pace or two back and forward as I tried to put order into all this question and answer. Then, when I thought I had it clear in my mind, I said,

"So what you are telling me is this. The murder of Darnley was just the first step in a plot to bring the Queen down. Bothwell, and Bothwell's ambition to marry the Queen, was the tool in that. And it was Moray who was the real force behind it all. Is that it?"

George turned from me again without making any answer; but his silence was answer enough. I let the silence endure for a moment before I asked, "And the danger to the Queen now?"

George's head whipped round to me as if it had been pulled on a string. "Can you not guess? The whole country accepts now that Bothwell is guilty of Darnley's murder, even although he has never been legally declared so. But once Moray manages to turn all the talk about him into an official declaration of guilt, how long do you think the Queen can escape being charged with the same crime?"

I stared in horror at him. He was shaking. The face that normally looked so smooth and handsome was transformed by his distress to an ugly mask. "And I love her!" The voice that came out of the mask had a strangled sound. "Oh my God, how I love her!"

I gave him a moment or two to recover himself before I asked, "How will Moray go about this – making a legal charge against Bothwell, I mean?"

"He will convene a Parliament – bring witnesses to testify before it. And," George added bitterly, "you can depend on it he would have done so already if it had not been for the need to prepare the statements of these witnesses. But torture, you see, takes time."

I found myself inwardly flinching from the picture conjured up by those final words. And George, it seemed, had had enough of our conversation. He began clambering into the boat. I leaned on the gunwale to steady it; and as he picked up the oars, I asked,

"How long have you known all this about Moray? Since the Queen was first brought here?"

"Known!" George gave a little laugh. "That is the wrong word, Will. No-one *knows* anything about Moray. That is his strength. He orders his lieutenants – men like Lindsay – in hints, and half-hints.

And as for those outside that charmed circle, they just have to guess and piece small things together – slowly, as I have done – before they can finally arrive at the truth."

"But George –" I kept my hold on the gunwale, unwilling to let George go until I had the last piece of the puzzle about Moray in place, " – why does he hate the Queen so? He must hate her, if all you say of him is true."

George shook his head. "You do not understand," he said. "Moray does not hate her. The Queen is right, in fact, to claim that he loves her. But what she has not recognised is that he loves power even more. And he had that, you see, so long as she leaned on *him* for advice – which she did, always. Until she married Darnley, that is; and then he lost all influence over her. But that was also when he discovered it was no use to fight back openly against the marriage – you remember?"

I nodded. I had been little more than a child at the time, of course; but even a child could not have failed to be impressed by the events of that time. Moray in the field with one army, the Queen at the head of her own troops opposing him – the excitement in the Castle had been tremendous then!

"Then you will remember too," George said, "how brilliantly the Queen defeated *that* bid for power. But this at least you can say for Moray. He learns from his mistakes – learns well too; because these more devious methods that got him the Regency will bring him more now than power. He will have money from them too – much money; all the rich pickings to be had from administering the Royal estates of the Queen's little son. And it is to safeguard both kinds of gain, now, that the Queen must be branded with Bothwell's guilt. Not only dethroned, you see, but ultimately destroyed as well."

I had heard enough. I let the boat go then – indeed, George gave such a shove of the oars on his final word, that I could not have held it longer. I stood watching him pull across to the mainland, feeling a great pity for the Queen walking so blindly into the trap that had been set for her. And still too trusting to see the danger it held. Because what was it Arnault had said? "*Her faith in her own innocence of any crime is too strong for that.*"

The loch grew wilder yet with the sleet battering on it. I turned away from its heaving grey water and walked towards the Castle, feeling cold now from more than the winter wind driving on my back.

11

That cold November was followed by a brief spell of most peculiar weather – certain days of a humid calm quite unnatural to the season. It was just before the middle of December that this spell began; the very same time as Sir William had word that Moray was once more coming to see the Queen. And for the three days between that advance notice and Moray's actual arrival, I could feel the effect of this odd weather adding to the general air of uneasiness in the Castle.

The Queen herself, in fact, was the only one who seemed untouched by this uneasiness. With an appearance of total composure she listened to Sir William telling her the nature of Moray's visit, stressing all the while how formal this was intended to be; and calmly, when the explanation was finished, she said,

"Very well, Sir William. You may make it known to Moray and his party of lords that I will grant them an audience."

I gawked at the form of this announcement, as much as Sir William did; but there was still another surprise in store for us.

"In the Presence Chamber," the Queen added. "You may bring them to me there."

Sir William looked helplessly at her. It was she herself, certainly, who had ordered a Presence Chamber to be built in Lochleven. But that had been when she was a reigning Monarch, entitled to such dignities. But now she knew – had he not just been at pains to impress it on her? – the reason for Moray's visit. A Parliament had at last been held. And the proceedings Moray had brought before that Parliament had confirmed the very fears George had voiced for her. Yet here she was, after months of seemingly tame acceptance of Moray's Regency, suddenly reasserting her Royal rights over him!

There was no denying, either, that she meant to have these. Coldly she listened to Sir William's protests. As coldly, she dismissed them with a swift reminder of the way she had been forced to sign the Deed of Abdication; and suddenly, then, I thought I understood what lay behind her attitude.

She had seen the danger! She had accepted at last that the net cast for Bothwell was closing on her also. And she was determined to give Moray open challenge on that!

"Did you convince her of it?" I asked George. "Or did she come to it of her own accord?"

"Half and half," George admitted. "That day I talked to you about it, Will – I pulled off from the landing-stage then, knowing that I *had* to make her see it. And praise God, she became gradually more and more amenable to argument."

"So she'll wait no longer for aid from France?"

"No – praise God again! She is ripe and ready for

escape, with as little delay now as possible."

I felt my heart give a most tremendous leap of excitement. In a rush of words I exclaimed, "Then I can get her out! I have been thinking and thinking ever since the last time we spoke of it, and I am certain now that there is only one way to get over all the difficulties. *She must walk openly out of the Castle*."

George stared in disbelief. "Have you lost your wits?"

"No, I have found them! I shall need some help in the plan, of course; but only from Minny, and only at the beginning of it. The rest will be up to the Queen herself, then. And so listen – "

I went on speaking as rapidly as I could in my efforts to convince George. But I was still not making sufficient impression. I could see that all the time I talked; and disappointment rose sharply in me when he said finally.

"It could succeed, I suppose. But there are so many "ifs" to it . . ."

"So you will not let me try it – is that what you mean?"

"No, no, you are leaping ahead," George reproved. "It does have some merits. And if we are forced eventually to rely on it, then I suppose we must. But that will only happen, remember, if I am not here myself to think of a better plan."

The lump of disappointment in my throat suddenly vanished. With cold alarm creeping in to replace it, I asked, "Why do you talk like that? Is it – Is it Moray? Has he begun to suspect you?"

George shrugged. "How could he fail to suspect? I have continued to carry the Queen's letters to him, after all; and so he knows my sympathy for her. Besides, there is gossip and guesswork all over the country about our life here in Lochleven. And Moray has spies everywhere – including the one in our very midst. Or had you forgotten about Drysdale?"

Captain Drysdale – I *had* forgotten about him! "But you said yourself," I protested, "that Sir William would keep quiet over the business with the barge. You said he would have to, in case it had a bad effect on his own position here."

"True," George agreed. "But what had Drysdale to lose by telling Moray of it? And you know what a grasping creature Drysdale has always been where money is concerned. What did he stand to gain by way of a bribe for information supplied?"

And Drysdale also hated the Queen! The cold feeling of alarm began to reach right through me. I said quickly, "You should get away – clear out altogether while Moray is here. There would be nothing, then, to remind Moray of his suspicions."

"Maybe so," George agreed. "On the other hand, to run might be to admit guilt. But I *will* lie low, I promise you. And Moray, when he comes here to-morrow, will not find anything that draws his eye to me."

I wanted to take George's word for that; wanted most anxiously to do so. But George, I remembered gloomily, was Commander of the Castle Guard. And that would bring him very much under Moray's eye – would it not? – when his soldiers had to escort the Queen to the Presence Chamber.

It stood apart from the Castle's main tower – a single-storied building with its doorway in the gable end facing the courtyard, a large window high up in the gable built into the courtyard wall. The one room inside this building was a spacious, vaulted chamber, unfurnished except for a throne-like chair of red velvet placed on the dais beneath the large window. Sir William inspected it on the morning of the day Moray was due – yet another of those oddly-calm days; and then fretted away the next few hours with complaints that Moray would blame *him* for the Queen's insistence on using it.

At two o'clock the soldier on lookout duty came hurrying to tell him that Moray's party had been sighted approaching the mainland landing-stage. George was given his orders to escort the Queen to the Presence Chamber, and Sir William went down to our own west landing-stage to greet Moray. There he stood with one hand on my shoulder as he watched the approaching boats; and even if I had not known how nervous he was by that time, the strength of his grip would have told me so.

"She will ruin me yet, Will," he muttered. "Do you know that? She will ruin me!"

It came to me with some force then that it was *I* who could be the instrument of his ruin, and I was more dismayed than I could have believed possible. Sir William had never been less than kind to me, after all, despite the occasional beatings I had suffered from him. I found myself reaching up my own hand to cover the one holding my shoulder. Sir William looked down at this, then drew me close to him; and I was still gripped by the feeling this roused in me when the boats with Moray's party in them touched at the landing-stage.

Moray was sombre in black again, but the numerous lords who were with him this time were peacocked out in reds and blues and silvers, glittered with jewelled rings and the gold of neck-chains, plumed with feathered hats that matched the glowing colours of their velvet doublets. I was swamped in a sea of colour, deafened by a rumble of voices, pushed and jostled from Sir William's side as they all crowded around him and Moray.

The rumble became shot through with individual cries of protest as the crowding men caught the drift of the conversation between these two. I made out Lord Lindsay's voice among those that cried loudest; and once more I heard the ugly epithets he had used of the Queen at her own landing there. And that decided me. I knew for certain now how false these were. And as for my feelings towards Sir William, *he* had never acknowledged me as his son. It was the Queen who had drawn the sting that word "bastard" had so often dealt me. I would not weaken towards Sir William again, I vowed; not so long as she had only George and myself to stand between her and the fate *this* mob had planned!

The party fell into place behind Moray leading them towards the Castle gate, and I regained my accustomed place at Sir William's heels. From halfway across the courtyard, I saw that the door to the Presence Chamber stood open. Lined up outside it were the soldiers of the Queen's escort, with George Douglas commanding them to attention. The voices of Moray's party died away as we neared the door, until the only sound breaking the odd stillness of that day was the tramp of our own feet. We crowded into the Presence Chamber, Moray still in the lead, Sir William behind him, myself behind Sir William.

The Queen was standing beside the red velvet chair in the pose that was usual for her – one hand on the back of the chair, the other fingering her gold crucifix hanging on its slender golden neckchain. She was in black, slashed with purple, and her head was crowned with light from the window behind her. She made no move at the sight of the crowding lords. As the last man entered, the voice of George Douglas came from beyond the door, with an order to the soldiers to "*Stand easy*." And then, as suddenly as a stage-effect that had been carefully planned and practised, there was a moment I would not have believed if I had not been there myself to see it happen.

From the moveless air outside – the air that had not held a breath of wind for all of three days – came a blast so powerful that the lattice of the window behind the Queen was burst wide open. She swayed to the force of the blast. The gaudy group assembled before her swayed also, and opened mouths of superstitious terror. The Queen's grasp on her chair brought her quickly upright again; and with eyes sweeping contemptuously over all the gaping faces, she cried out,

"The heavens speak, my lords, and send a wind for traitors!"

Sir William rushed to the window and brought the wild flapping of the casement under control. "Yes, bolt it again," the Queen told him, "but treachery has already entered here!"

Moray stepped forward, clearing his throat. "Your Grace – " he began. "Sister – "

Fiercely the Queen rounded on him. "You call me "sister" and I always have been a sister to you, heaping love and favours on you, pardoning your former rebellion, forgiving every act that was not the act of a brother. But what have your actions been to me, my lord? – for I will never call you "brother" again. How have you treated me?"

"Your Majesty – " Moray tried again, but still the

Queen would not let him speak.

"Yes, my Majesty! And what have you tried to do against that, Moray? I have asked you often enough for the freedom I should justly have. I have asked even more often for something I value far more highly than freedom – the chance to appear before the Privy Council to defend myself against the vile innuendoes cast on me. But you, unjust and base as you are, have acted in every way towards me as an enemy. Because do not think, my lord, that I am now as ignorant as I once was of the meaning behind all your manoeuvres – your sly off-going to France, leaving behind you a rebellion already plotted, your delay in first coming to visit me here in my prison, *And* the reason also for your even longer delay in convening the Parliament that has now confirmed the outlawry of the Earl Bothwell, stripped him of all his offices and dignities, laid him under pain of treason, and declared him guilty of murder.

"You needed time to bring me down with him, time to manufacture the "evidence" that would link *my* name to murder also, and so justify my continued imprisonment here. And time also, my lord, to persuade Parliament to confirm that you and these other lords should have indemnity for all your treacherous actions."

It was magnificent, I thought. *She* was magnificent, poised there like some young storm-goddess in the trail of that violent wind. And all her accusations were hitting home to Moray. He was staring at her, clearly aghast at the degree of truth in her tirade – but was it wise to humiliate him so completely? And in front of all that assembly of lords, too! One of them – the Earl of Morton – had stepped to Moray's side now, and was feebly trying to pacify her.

"Your Grace," he pleaded, "my lord Moray was appointed Regent at the instance of the Council. And it *is* as the Council that we come here now to inform you of Parliament's decisions. As to your freedom, I personally will do everything in my power – "

"You *have* no power!" Sharp as a scythe cutting through corn, the Queen cut through Morton's words. "You are Moray's creature. You are all his creatures. And I would rather wear out my life in perpetual imprisonment than accept freedom now at his hands."

She paused, looked directly at Moray, and then let her eyes travel over the other faces there. Moray did not return her look, and he did not try to take advantage of the pause to speak again. I wondered why. Was it rage that tied his tongue? Or astonishment that so gentle a nature could suddenly show such force? Or was he simply too taken aback, still, by her knowledge, to even try some denial of its truth?

"My lords – " The Queen's eyes had returned to Moray, and she was speaking more quietly now. " – I vow this to you. I shall never again speak face to face with the Earl of Moray. *But I shall regain my freedom*! And as there is a just God in heaven, that freedom will be to Moray's disgrace, damage, and ruin."

Proudly then she stepped down from her place on the dais and walked straight towards Moray. Still without looking at her, he moved a step to let her pass. But the Queen did not pass. Instead, she stopped and looked intently at his averted face, at the hands that seemed to hang nerveless at his sides. Then, in one swift movement, she had hold of one of these hands in a gesture that forced his eyes to hers.

"You will repent your perfidy to me!" Her voice

was breaking now, with tears barely restrained; but she mastered the break, and finished, "Sooner or later, and cost what it might, I tell you that you shall repent!"

The lords gave way in silence before her as she continued her proud exit from the Presence Chamber. She had been right – they *were* all Moray's creatures. And where she had so thoroughly asserted herself as still having Sovereign right over him, there was none of them – not even one so brash as Lord Lindsay – who would dare to challenge her . . .

"She has some informant here, I tell you!"
Moray's voice, as he faced Sir William in the Great Hall, was nearer to a snarl than to human speech. "She knew too much about me *not* to have an informant. And I know who it is, d'ye hear? *I know!*"

He glared all around him – at Sir William, at Lady Agnes, the Old Lady; even at myself. There was no-one else there. The lords had been dismissed, back to their boats; for this, it seemed, was to be a family inquisition.

"Now, James – " the Old Lady began soothingly; but Moray ignored her. Head lowered like that of a bull about to charge, his very beard quivering with anger, he fixed his glare finally on Sir William, and roared.

"But you will banish him from this place! I command it. Banish George Douglas from Lochleven – or I will have him *hanged!*"

Lady Agnes screamed. The Old Lady gasped. Even Sir William flinched from the impact of Moray's final word. Moray ignored the women. With his gaze still on Sir William, he went on.

"As for you, you have been much too lenient with her, or she could not have written the letters George carried to me. But that must end. You will seize all her writing materials, or answer to me for it. And mark this, brother; mark it well. If she does escape, as she claims she will do, you will answer to me for that too!"

Abruptly, on this, he turned on his heel and stalked from the room. The quivering silence he left behind was broken by a sob from Lady Agnes. The Old Lady shook herself out of what seemed an almost trance-like state and began wildly to babble that her Geordie was innocent of all harm; that nothing and nobody was going to take him away from her. Sir William turned to me.

"Fetch George here," he ordered nervously. "And for God's sake, boy, be quick about it."

With a hand pushing in the small of my back, he thrust me to the door. I took the flight of steps outside it in a series of bounds, then raced for the likeliest place to find George. He was where I had guessed – in the barracks; and as fast as I could, I told him my story. But George was not so shaken by it as I had expected.

"I was fairly sure it would come to this," he told me, "after the way the Queen spoke in the Presence Chamber."

"You heard it all?"

"Every word. The door was left open – remember? And her voice carried well. But I still cannot leave here. Not now. Not with matters at this stage."

I looked in bewilderment at him. "But you have no choice! I told you, George. Sir William has been *ordered* to banish you."

"Ah, yes." George gave the beginnings of a smile.

"Sir William has been ordered. But who really orders Sir William? And what if I plead so prettily with the Old Lady that she cannot find it in her heart to let my brother send me away from her?"

"Even if she knows the danger you would be in then?"

"I could persuade her otherwise, I think." George was speaking half to himself now, working out his ideas as he did so. "It will be very hard for the Old Lady to accept that any of her sons could deliberately kill his brother . . ."

"But supposing you did manage to persuade her of that," I argued. "And supposing *she* managed to persuade Sir William to let you stay. The danger would be no less real, would it not?"

The smile slid away from George's face. "I will have to be taken before I am hanged," he told me; "which means I shall just have to keep one step ahead of Moray's men. And so, come on, Will. You were told to hurry back with me."

I fell into step with him across the courtyard. Together we mounted the steps to the Great Hall, then I stood aside to let him enter ahead of me. The Old Lady and Sir William both rose at the sight of him, and one glance at their faces told me of the argument they must have had while I was away. Sir William looked sullen now, rather than agitated; and although it took a lot to make the Old Lady weep, she *had* been weeping.

"Geordie!" she exclaimed, and held out her arms to him. George went swiftly to her, his own arms held out in reply; and as they came together in embrace, I had the feeling in my bones that there was only one way the argument could go now. George would be allowed to stay – for a time, at least. Yet it could not be all that long, I realised, before Moray discovered that his command had not been carried out. And so it looked very much as if George *would* be forced to rely on the escape plan I had put to him!

12

Carefully I began laying the groundwork my plan needed.

I would have little problem, I knew, in persuading Minny to give the help I wanted from her. If she would not, for the Queen's sake, do as I asked, she would do it for mine. But Minny, I soon discovered, was more than willing to be active in the Queen's cause. Minny had already heard the soldiers of the escort tell of the dressing-down she had given Moray. All the servants in the Castle, indeed, had heard their story. And Minny was delighted by it.

"Because," said she, "it is not only high time that Moray learned what it feels like to have his nose put out of joint. It goes against the grain, also, to see such continued injustice against the Queen."

I was intrigued by this. What did Minny know, after all, about affairs of State? "*I* know," I said, "that the stories about the Queen are false. I have good warrant for knowing. But how can you be so sure?"

Minny grinned at me, the impish grin that always made her look half her true age. "You have a poor memory, Will," she remarked. "Do you not recall how I checked Ellen for speaking slander about the Queen?"

I remembered that very well. "But," I added, "I remember also thinking then that you were doing no more than giving some of your usual common-sense advice."

"There was a bit more to it than that," Minny informed me. "I have noticed something about men, Will. Whenever they are jealous of any power a woman may have, they always go the same way about trying to drag her down – tarnishing her good name first, branding her with words like "whore", in the certain knowledge that some at least of the mud they fling, will stick. And that, I think, has been the fate of this poor Queen."

We were sobered by this, myself as much as Minny. I settled down immediately to telling her of the part I meant her to play; and once I had got her agreement to it, I went off to wait with what patience I could, for the result of this.

Minny had no news for me the next day; but that was because – for once – the Old Lady had not brought her maid across with her on her daily visit from the New House. And it was through Kirsty, the maid, that Minny would have to reach the Old Lady's ear. On the day following, however, we had better luck. Kirsty came with the Old Lady as usual, and Minny had the chance to send her message.

"And then," she reported gleefully, "I did just what you told me, Will. When the Old Lady came across to see me, I told her, I just told her straight, *"Well, your Ladyship, it has come to this. I cannot go on any longer with the extra burden of work that washing for the Queen and her ladies has put on me. My back is near to breaking with it all. And besides, there is the ironing of it –*

all those delicate laces and frills, it takes too long, altogether too long. So there it is, your Ladyship. I have made up my mind to take service with some other family that can be more kind to me – unless, of course, you can farm out all that extra work to someone else..."

"And what did she say to that?" I was laughing by then, the way Minny herself was laughing, but still thinking ahead to the next move. "What did she say?" I repeated, because Minny was not looking quite so triumphant now.

"Once a week," Minny said. "She would not agree to bringing in help more than once a week. But the arrangement is to start right away, Will. "*You can send a message over to some respectable woman in Kinross,*" she told me, "*and as soon as I have approved of her, she can start coming once a week to collect the linen from the Queen's apartments.*" And that is better than nothing, is it not?"

Once a week would suit my plan nicely, I thought; and Minny had done well, to fool someone as sharp as the Old Lady. I told her so, in the warmest of terms, and straight away started to get from her a note of all the washer women in Kinross.

I was surprised then, to find that such a small place could produce so many of these; but it was not just any woman who would do, of course, and so the list narrowed finally to the five that Minny reckoned might be worth my while to visit. But, I decided, I could not do all that in one trip to the mainland, since that would mean being too long absent from my duties with Sir William.

I would have to allow myself two days to make my choice among them. And meanwhile, there was George. He would need to be told that my plan was now at least under way; but I would have to be very careful how I went about that. Sir William had yielded very reluctantly to the Old Lady's insistence that George should be allowed to stay on in the Castle; and I might come under suspicion too, if he and I were now seen with our heads together.

I waited for my chance to speak privately to him, and found this the next morning when I saw him on his way to the north tip of the island – the place he most favoured for the flying of his hawks. I stalked him through the garden to that point, and had all the talk I wanted before I used the cover of the garden again to reach the east landing-stage and my own boat waiting there for me.

I was feeling very pleased with myself, accordingly, as I oared the boat swiftly towards the mainland and my search among the washerwomen of Kinross. George had been more amused than annoyed to know what I had done thus far. He had even admitted to a change of mind over the prospect of success for my plan. And not only that. He had actually gone so far as to say he would give official notice of it to John Beaton!

I pulled lustily for the mainland's public landing-stage, tied up my boat among the ferryboats waiting there for hire, and set off to find the houses of the five women on my list.

The luck that began that day for me did not last. Of the three women I managed to see before I had to go go back to the Castle, two already had all the work they could manage. The third – who had just the right height and build for my purpose – could not accept my offer because she had a sick child to look after. That brought me to the end of the time I could spare from my duties without the risk of Sir William noticing my absence; and so I had to resign myself to starting all over again on the following day.

I had no chance to speak again with George, either, before I did so. George, it seemed, had taken off early that morning for the mainland; and from the sour look of Sir William as he remarked on this, I was left in no doubt that he suspected the purpose of George's absence. I kept discreetly silent through all his grumbles on the subject, and tried to increase my own protection against suspicion by being more than ever attentive to him. His sour mood slowly lost its edge until he reached the point where he was ruffling my hair and telling me,

"You, at least, are a good lad, Will. *You* have the sense to know which side your bread is buttered."

"Yes, sir," I said humbly. "Thank you, sir." And obediently, when he ordered to do so, I entertained him with card tricks and played the fool long enough to turn his humour completely sweet again. I did all this with a reasonably good grace too, knowing very well how his relations with the Queen had cooled since her scene with Moray, and – in spite of myself – feeling some compassion for the way he was now denying himself the pleasures of her apartments.

So the greater part of that day vanished from beneath my grasp, until it was five o'clock in the afternoon, and almost dark. That still gave me two hours, however, before I had to serve Sir William's supper, and so I did not hesitate when the chance came to slip away from him. Within a quarter of an hour from that time I was tying up my boat again at the mainland stage, and hurrying off to search for the first of the two women still on my list.

Mistress Jean Lawson, she was called. She lived

only a few minutes away from the landing-stage, and the moment she answered my knock on her door I realised that luck could once more be with me. Mistress Lawson, I saw then, was an elderly woman, but she was still tall enough and thin enough for my purpose. Not only that, she was willing also to come straight away with me to the Castle, to be approved by the Old Lady.

"If you will just give me time to get my shawl," she said, "and to let my good man know where I have gone at such a darkling hour."

"With pleasure, mistress," I told her. "And I will wait for you at the landing-stage."

I strolled the hundred yards from her house to where my little boat bobbed beside the larger craft still waiting for hire. The streets of Kinross were dark and deserted now, and there were only two men left waiting beside their ferry boats. I talked idly with them until Mistress Lawson appeared beside me. They made some joking remarks to her then, but I cut this short; and seconds later, she was seated in my little boat while I rowed most cheerfully with her to the island.

I had covered half the distance there when we both became aware of some commotion on the landing-stage we had left so quiet behind us. I rested the oars momentarily, to look back; and dark as it was by then, I thought I could see a horse at the water's edge, with its rider in the act of dismounting.

"Someone in a hurry to find a boat-hire," Mistress Lawson remarked; and sure enough then, we both saw one of the ferry-boats pushing off from the landing-stage.

Could it be George? I bent to the oars again, and rowed at a quicker pace than before. The larger boat, with two men at the oars, began to pull up on me. I touched at the landing-stage only half a minute before they did, and leapt ashore with the mooring-rope in my hand. The passenger from the other boat came hard on my heels – and it was George. I called out to him. I heard him order his boatmen to wait for his return to the mainland. Then he closed with me; and low in my ear he said urgently,

"Moray has sent men to make sure the ban on me is enforced. And they are only half an hour behind me now. But I must see the Queen before they see Sir William. I *must*, Will."

"I can clear the coast for you." I spoke rapidly in reply, all the speculation that had been racing through my mind crystallising instantly into a plan of action. "This woman with me – we will use her as the decoy in that."

I turned quickly to my own boat, helped Mistress Lawson ashore, and told her, "Now, mistress, if you will just follow this gentleman and myself. . ."

George and I set off at a pace that might have been a little too brisk for her liking, but she came close enough behind us, for all that. "Mistress Jean Lawson, to see Lady Margaret Douglas," I told the sentries at the gate, nodding towards her. They let her pass, and as we walked across the courtyard, I told George the detail of my intentions.

At the foot of the outside stair leading up to the doorway of the Great Hall, George stood aside. I beckoned the woman to follow me up to the door; and George – as I had warned him he must do – fell in close behind her. Once through the door, I led her along behind the service screen, with George all the time following and keeping low behind the screen's solid lower half. I reached the entrance gap at the screen's south-eastern limit. There I stopped, pulling the woman to a halt with me so that our presence side by side in the gap would entirely block any view beyond it.

The Old Lady was in the Hall along with the two girls, all three of them with their heads together over the nightly report the girls had to make. I paused in the gap for the moment George would need to cross it behind cover of Mistress Lawson and myself, and thus gain the inner stair leading up to the Queen's apartments. Then, to the Old Lady I announced,

"This woman, Your Ladyship, is Mistress Jean Lawson. Minny sent me to fetch her to you."

Firmly I thrust Mistress Lawson forward; and myself turned towards the stairs. It was Lady Agnes who would be in the Queen's apartments at that hour. That was the likelihood behind all my calculations. But supposing Sir William was there too? The excuse that would get rid of Lady Agnes would certainly not do for him! I sped upwards, trying hard to figure some alternative device for getting him out of George's way.

Kerr and Newland, the two surly fellows guarding the Queen's door, stared stonily at me as I knocked there. Then their eyes went indifferently past me – as they must earlier have gone past the accustomed sight of George, mounting still higher up the stairs as if climbing towards the level of his own quarters. The voice of Lady Agnes answered my knock; and I went in to find her seated in a group with the Queen and the Queen's ladies, all four of them busy with their sewing. I made my bow to the Queen, and raised my head to say,

"If it please Your Grace..." Deliberately I held her gaze for seconds longer than was proper to this formality. I saw her eyes become suddenly alert before I turned to tell Lady Agnes,

"If Her Grace permits, Your Ladyship, there is a Mistress Lawson just arrived to seek employment as a washerwoman. Minny sent me to Kinross to fetch her."

"But surely – " Lady Agnes looked at me in some puzzlement. "There must be some mistake, Will. *I* know nothing of any Mistress Lawson."

"Then perhaps," the Queen suggested gently, "you had better find out."

"Er – well, yes. With Your Grace's permission." Lady Agnes rose in a flustered sort of way, and made her curtsy to the Queen. I sprang to open the door for her, and followed her to the stairs, calling loudly after her the "all-clear" signal that would be heard by George waiting in the half-dark of the landing one flight above me.

"*In the Hall, Your Ladyship. The woman is waiting in the Great Hall.*"

"Come here to me, Will." The Queen's voice summoned me back into the room, and I hurried to her. She and her ladies had thrust aside their sewing, and I could see from their faces that she *had* guessed there was something in the wind.

"Pray, Your Grace – " I blurted the words out over her questions, "waste no time. Mr George is closely pursued by Moray's men, and he must see you. This is his last, his very last chance – "

"Your Grace!" George's entrance, George's exclamation, interrupted me. In swift strides he was across the room and going down on one knee before the Queen. "I have gathered all the latest intelligence from John Beaton," he told her; "and here is the burden of it. Moray has over-reached himself with his Parliament, and opinion in the country is now veering in your favour. The common people, Beaton reports, are content to see Bothwell pursued with all the rigours of the law, but they do not want to see *you* further hounded. They want their Queen returned to them, Your Grace. They have become uneasy at your continued imprisonment – "

"And the lords?" Her face in a glow of delight, the Queen broke in. "What support can I expect there?"

"All that you formerly had. Huntly, Arbroath, Galloway, Ross, Fleming, Herries – "George went on reeling off a list of names that ended with, " – and chiefest of all, of course, your old friend Lord Seton. But besides that, some of the lords who *were* on Moray's side are now talking of supporting you instead – even some of those who were here with him, less than a week ago. They have become uneasy, it seems, at the power Moray now has. And so Lord Seton has sent me to ask your permission to assure all these of your renewed favour, if they do return to their proper allegiance."

"Lord Seton shall have it, Mr Douglas. I will write to him now!" The Queen jumped to her feet, rushed to her desk – and then remembered! There, at least, Moray had been obeyed; and Sir William had been thorough in raiding her supply of writing materials. The only remnant of these was a pen – an old one with its quill all broken – that had been left on her desk as being too battered for further use. With some vague thought of lending a hand in this crisis. I drew my knife to try sharpening its point. But the Queen was already far ahead of me. Snatching up the empty inkwell from her desk, she thrust it into Jane Kennedy's hands.

"Soot from the fireplace," she commanded. "And you, Maria, fetch water."

Kennedy rushed to scrape soot into the inkwell. de Courcelles ran to the bed-chamber. I kept on sharpening the point of the quill, stealing glances all the while. Now Kennedy was coming back to the desk to place the inkwell on it. de Courcelles was running back from the bed-chamber, a little jug of water in her hand. The Queen had picked up the largest of her tapestry needles, and was standing ready for them both.

de Courcelles handed the water to her. She tipped some of it in among the soot, mixed the result swiftly and thoroughly with her tapestry needle, then took her handkerchief of fine white lawn from the cuff of her gown, and spread it out on the desk before her.

"Listen at the door," she commanded Kennedy and de Courcelles. They ran to crouch down with heads pressed against the door, while she seated herself and said, "Now the pen. And keep firm hold of this while I write."

I handed her the pen; and from my side of the desk, I steadied the top and bottom right-hand corners of the handkerchief. George did the same for the left-hand side, so that the white square of stuff lay taut and flat on the desk before her. She wrote her message – a mere six lines; and then, in her bold Italian hand, the signature "*Marie R.*" Our hands released the white square, and the Queen laid down her pen.

"I will signal to you, Your Grace," George told her, "to let you know this has been delivered. Look out for me when you walk in the garden. I shall ride my horse out into the water of the mainland shore, and come as close as I dare."

"And my escape?" she asked. "Is there a plan for that?"

George nodded towards me. "Will has something in hand. He will tell you of it himself. And trust him, I beg you. He is loyal."

Surprise – or was it doubt? – showed briefly on the Queen's face; but she did not voice her feelings. Instead, she reached up quickly to take off one of her earrings – one of the pear-shaped pearls that were her favourite jewels. With her fingers working on it, she told George,

"Then take my letter to Lord Seton with the hope that I shall soon be leading my forces in person." The pearl was loose now. She held it out to George with one hand, gave him the handkerchief with the other, and added, "And when the moment comes to receive me on the mainland, send this pearl back to me as a signal that all is ready there."

George stowed the pearl and the handkerchief inside his doublet, speaking as he did so. "I will do more than that, Your Grace. The boy's plan may fail. In which case, we must think of another, and perhaps yet another. But when I send the pearl back it will be not only the sign that we are ready for you. It will tell you also that matters have reached the point for an escape plan that *must not* fail."

Swiftly then he knelt to add, "And so, Your Grace, adieu. And, as God hears me, I shall be your true and faithful servant until death."

The Queen opened her mouth to reply; and in the same moment came a cry from the listeners at the door, "Hush! Oh, hush!"

George was on his feet on the instant, his head

turned in a listening attitude. Everyone listened, breath held, bodies motionless. Footsteps! We could all hear them now – faint, but rapidly growing louder; the footsteps of a number of men coming quickly up the stairs. George moved to the door. I whispered urgently,

"You'll be killed!"

"Not I! I'll fight my way through!" He was at the door, his hand on the latch. Over his shoulder he threw a last word to the Queen. "*Trust the boy!*"

The noise of footsteps had a voice added to it by then, Sir William's voice loudly roaring George's name. I made to follow him as he plunged through the doorway, but the Queen's hand restrained me. Her eyes were big with fright. For her letter? For George's life? I was frightened only for George at that moment.

We could hear the muffled sound of two men's voices now – George and Sir William, each trying to outshout the other; but it was Sir William's voice that finally over-topped the general din of accusation and counter-accusation.

" – and think yourself lucky I have not shot you with my own hand, instead of standing between you and Moray's men. But I *will* shoot you, if you do not take yourself instantly out of Lochleven. I will have the Castle cannon turned on you, by God, if you come within half a mile of here again!"

A sound of footsteps descending the stairs, and voices that faded as the footsteps faded; there was nothing more to be heard after that. George was finally banished – but he had at least escaped with his life. I let out a long, shivering breath of relief. The Queen and her ladies did so too. The Queen's eyes met mine; and with a little smile that seemed oddly sad to me, she said,

"So, Will Douglas, I am in your hands now."

"'An it please Your Grace." It was the force of realising the truth of this, rather than good manners,
that brought me down on one knee before her then.
"I will be your saviour, Your Grace, if you will let
me."

"My little orphan," she asked, "why should I not?
I *have* no help now, except you."

"And no-one, Your Grace, who is more loyal to
you."

She held out her hand to me as I said this. I dared to
take the hand in my own, and to kiss it – just as
George had done when he first swore allegiance to
her. And just as had happened with me then, I had a
feeling I could not place. I looked up into the Queen's
face. She was still wearing that oddly sad little smile;
and suddenly I knew the nature of my feeling. I had
lost something, I realised. I had lost my envy of
George.

13

The Queen was as charmed by my plan as I was myself.

I had been careful, after all, to make sure that Mistress Lawson resembled her in height and build; and the guards would soon become used to seeing the woman come weekly to the Castle. Kerr and Newland would have their instructions to let her enter the Queen's apartments to collect and deliver the linen for washing; and once that pattern had been well established, the rest would follow quickly.

A sufficient bribe to make the favour worth her while, and Mistress Lawson could be persuaded to lend the Queen her dress and shawl. With these for disguise, then, the shawl pulled well forward to hide her features and a bundle of linen tucked under her arm, there would be nothing to stop the Queen walking calmly out of her apartments and down to the boat awaiting the return of the "washerwoman" to the mainland.

That was more or less the sum of it; and the moment I learned from Minny that Mistress Lawson's employment had been confirmed, the Queen was anxious to write letters that would arrange the events to follow her escape. Lady Agnes, however, was now too far gone with child to be nimble in thieving further supplies for writing the supposed "journal", and so it was I who did so. The Queen wrote her letters during her supper-hour – the only time she was allowed to sit in private; and then, with these hidden alongside a further letter that would be my credential as her courier, I went ashore to see if I could find John Beaton.

I was nervous, at first, about this – perhaps unreasonably so; but it was still only on the previous day that George had kept his promise to signal the safe delivery of the handkerchief letter and Sir William had acted on his threat to turn the Castle cannon on him. I kept low in my boat, thinking of the panic this had caused – especially in the Old Lady. That had upset me – but still not nearly so much as the sight of the cannon-shot whistling towards George. I tried to console myself by remembering that Drysdale's eagerness to train the guns had been the cause of the shots going wide of their mark. And I could not become the target either for Sir William's anger or Drysdale's spite, I argued, until I too became suspect. I had an uncomfortable journey all the same, and was still shaking a little from the effect of it by the time I had tied up my boat and was heading for the Kinross Inn.

It was Muriel, the black-eyed daughter of the house, who brought back my self-esteem. I deliberately sought her out there as the person least likely to report my doings, and discovered from her that Beaton had taken up almost permanent residence at the Inn.

"Although he keeps himself very much to himself," she added. And she smiled as she spoke, that demurely-enticing smile she knew I never could resist. I kissed her soundly then, without any noticeable resistance on her part; and with my faith in myself once more high in consequence of this, I followed her along the passage that led to Beaton's room.

No voice answered my knock on its door; and the door itself, I found, was locked. I bent to the keyhole and softly called my name. A key rattled in the lock, and Beaton opened to me. He looked just as I remembered him – lean, elegant, and wary-eyed as ever. Without a word of greeting he re-locked the door, then took the letters I handed him and began to scan the unsealed one that was my credential from the Queen. I glanced around the room as he read.

It was small, and sparsely furnished. One narrow pallet bed, two chairs, a small writing-desk – that was all it held. Its situation was on the ground floor. The lattice of its window stood open, in spite of the freezing weather outside, and opposite the open window was the doorway of the Inn's stables. It flashed through my mind that Beaton had made very sure he would not be trapped there by an unfriendly visitor. Then I became aware that his gaze had lifted from the letter to fix on me.

"So!" He tapped the letter with the fingers of his free hand. "You are the Queen's new courier, eh? And she has accepted the plan of escape you have worked out for her."

"That," I said boldly, "is because it will succeed. It is too simple, sir, *not* to succeed."

"Let me be the judge of that," Beaton advised. "And since the whole process of mustering an army will depend on it, I must have more detail than Mr Douglas could give when he told me of it."

I explained my plan, then, as fully as I could. It would be no problem, I pointed out, for the Queen to be secret in making the exchange of clothes with Mistress Lawson. The hour of the woman's visit had been fixed for ten o'clock in the morning, and it was well known to everyone that the Queen always stayed late abed. Ellen and Margaret would therefore have been up for hours while she was still lying in her bed-chamber; and that meant she would be alone there when Mistress Lawson arrived to collect the linen. But Maria de Courcelles would follow, when the woman went into the bed-chamber. Maria would help to speed the exchange of dress between them. And when the "washerwoman" finally departed again with her bundle, Maria would still be heard from the bed-chamber in apparent conversation with the "Queen".

As for how long it would be before all this could happen, five or six visits from Mistress Lawson, I had reckoned, would be sufficient for everyone – and not least the guards – to cease paying any attention to her entering and leaving the Queen's apartments. "And that," I finished, "would bring us to the 4th of February. Or, to be completely safe, we could say the 11th."

Beaton had begun to smile as I spoke; and with a rather caustic note of humour then, he said, "You have the makings of a spymaster in you, I see. And the plan is certainly feasible. But the timing of the escape must still relate to the weather conditions that will follow; and also to the question of our being able to bring superior numbers to the field."

I was dismayed. I had been so determined there would be no further shilly-shallying over freeing the Queen. Not now that *I* was in charge. Firmly I said,

"If you are thinking of the pleas the Queen has made for aid from France –"

"I am," Beaton interrupted, "but only in the sense that France's failure to help makes it all the more important for us to be able to muster superior numbers from our own resources. And we cannot be sure of doing that until we are sure also of yet another of the lords now wavering in his allegiance to Moray – no less a person, in fact, that the Earl of Argyll."

"*Argyll*!" I stared in disbelief. "But he is Moray's own brother-in-law!"

"Exactly. And that should show you how the opposition is now crumbling! What is more, Argyll can bring a greater number to the field than any of the other lords. He could bring us up to an army of six thousand, in fact – more than Moray could ever hope to raise. But he is cunning, a most cunning man. We need more time yet to bring him to a firm promise of support. And so what do you think now, my lad, of that escape date you gave me?"

I was not anxious to say what I thought, but could see no help for it. "I suppose," I admitted, "that I will have to be guided by your choice."

Beaton sketched me a bow. "In that case," he said, "we will forward the date of the Queen's escape to the 25th of March – thus giving ourselves not only the time we need to work on Argyll, but also the advantage of Spring weather for the opening of our campaign. Agreed?"

That last question, it seemed, was only a formality before he sat down at his desk and began to write. I waited in silence till he had finished. He sealed his letter, took a packet of other letters from his desk, then looked up at me.

"Just one more point then, Will. About this

Mistress Lawson on whom so much depends. Are you quite, quite sure she will fall in with your plan?"

Beaton had been too long away from the Queen's company, I thought. He seemed to have forgotten how her charm worked on everyone – witness the Court of Dreams! I smiled at my own recollection of this, and told him,

"I am quite, quite sure that the Queen can persuade Mistress Lawson to do so. And besides, Her Grace is generous in her rewards."

I gave ·him just a glimpse then, of the gold the Queen has insisted I should have for *my* services; but he frowned at this, and said sharply,

"Put it away!"

I slid the gold out of sight. He handed his letters to me, and went on, "Hide these too, until you can give them to the Queen. This newly-written one also, where I have explained the reasoning behind the choice of date for her escape."

I put the letters inside my doublet; but I had no intention of ending our interview on that note. I had a question to ask him; one that had been burning in my mind, and I meant at least to try for an answer to it.

"Er – and can you tell me, sir," I ventured, "if George Douglas is still unharmed? And also, perhaps, where he has hidden himself?"

Beaton gave me the wariest look I had yet had from him. Then, to my utter surprise, he said, "Will, I have learned from George that you feel tenderly for the Old – for Lady Margaret Douglas. But you do understand, do you not, that you could not give her any information now about George without betraying your own involvement in the Queen's affairs?"

He had caught me out so completely in this that I could only stammer. "I am sorry. She has been so concerned about him, you see. And I, too –"

"Have been just as concerned," Beaton finished for me. "But there is no need to worry, either on her behalf or on your own. I do assure you of that. George *is* in a safe hiding-place. And this very day, as it happens, he has sent a message to his mother to tell her so."

I let out a sigh of relief at this. It had not been comfortable, living with the Old Lady's distress over George; and if it had not been for Beaton's cautious attitude, I realised, I could have allowed that to lead me into a considerable blunder. I saw him smiling a little at my expression, and was encouraged then, to say,

"I take your meaning completely, sir; but – is there some chance, perhaps, that I might see George again before the date of the escape?"

Beaton shrugged. "It is possible, I suppose – *if* one of his visits to me here happens to coincide with your further courier work for the Queen."

"And if the Queen herself asks when she will see him again?"

"Tell her," Beaton said, "that the day she sets foot on the mainland, she will be met by an escort of fifty young gentlemen under the command of Lord Seton. And that George Douglas will be one of the fifty."

I left him with this and hurried from the Inn, resisting the temptation to see Muriel on my way out. The number "fifty" was echoing in my mind, and I rowed back to the Castle with my thoughts making it up to fifty-one. Because, I vowed to myself, I would be a member of that company! As soon as I saw the boat with the Queen in it touch at the mainland landing-stage, I would set out in my own little boat to join them. But to make sure I *could* do that, I would first of all have to create an excuse for being at our own landing-stage at the time she left from there . . .

Sir William was pleased when I began a regular weekly check of all our boats. "You are improving, Will," he told me. "You used not to be so conscientious in your duties."

"It saves time in the end," I said modestly; and continued to go down to the west landing-stage every Wednesday morning just before the time Mistress Lawson was due to arrive there. I stayed until she left again, around half an hour later; and made a point, meanwhile, of noting small things that might later be of use to the Queen. Finally, when I thought I had the whole situation well surveyed and there was a chance to talk without being overheard, I relayed my information to her.

"The woman's boat," I reported, "comes in always at the most convenient point – our west landing-stage. And she has no regular boatman. She just takes whichever one happens to be free for hire. Also, before she embarks on her return journey, she makes a habit of throwing her bundle ahead of her into the boat."

"She is not the talkative kind either," the Queen murmured. "And so – thank God – I shall not have to speak with any of those hired boatmen."

"But she is talking to you, is she not? I mean, you have managed to –" I stopped, as the Queen began smiling at this.

"But of course, Will. Gold is a great loosener of tongues!"

"And she *has* agreed to do as you ask?"

"Most certainly. She would have done so, I think, even without the bribe!"

So here, I thought, was at least some proof that George had not been mistaken in the intelligence he had risked so much to bring. First Minny, and now Mistress Lawson – the signs indeed were that the Queen was regaining the sympathy of the common people ... I sensed eyes on me at that point, and looked up to see Margaret Lindsay's gaze fixed on myself and the Queen. Immediately then, I felt uneasy.

Margaret Lindsay seemed always to be watching the Queen, these days – and not furtively, either, in the way that was called for by her role as a spy. There had been a change in that; a change I could date from the moment she had led her mother as the first of the Porches to make their curtsy to the Queen. And now, it seemed to me, Margaret's constantly-following gaze had a dog-like devotion in it. She had got even thinner, too, since that time of the Porches' visit; and her sallow face now bore a look of strain on it. I had begun to fancy, too, that the eyes in that face turned hostile whenever they rested on me alone; and I did not like the feeling this gave.

I made an excuse to rise and get away from the uncomfortable effect she had on me. But Margaret spoke suddenly, in a voice that seemed high and thin, compared to her usual tones.

"I dreamed. Last night I dreamed such a dream of you, Will Douglas!" Her eyes had shifted from the Queen's face, to mine. There was a sort of fixed stare to them; and both her look and her words gave me a chill that was like fear. But what had I to fear from Margaret Lindsay?

"You brought a bird into the Castle, in my dream." Still in those high tones, she went on; and still she stared. "A big, black bird it was, like a raven. But it was bigger than a raven. It was enormous. It followed you, flying after you. And then it swooped down to seize the Queen, and flew off with her. With my Queen!"

Her hands released the sewing they held. It slid off her lap, to the floor. The hands hovered, empty, for a moment. Then one of them jerked upwards, to cover her mouth. From behind the covering hand came in a muffled scream,

"With *my* Queen!"

The sound had the room instantly in a stir, with Ellen shrinking back from Margaret, the Queen and her ladies starting towards her. She was rocking and moaning now, as if in some sort of fit; but when the Queen knelt to soothe her, the moaning turned to a quiet weeping that was quite pitiful to witness. The Queen grasped both of the girl's hands in her own and said gently,

"You are not well, child. You cannot be well, or you would not have such dreams."

Words began to come through the sound of weeping, broken words, fitfully uttered. I thought I heard "escape" among them, and "leaving me". The Queen's hearing was sharper than mine – or else it was her closeness to Margaret that allowed her to hear more distinctly. She clasped the girl's hands more tightly, and told her,

"But of course I shall escape. I must! And so must Kennedy and de Courcelles. We shall all leave here. But listen to me now. This is what we shall do –"

Briefly, over Margaret's shoulder, her eyes warned me to make myself scarce; then she bent closer yet to the girl and began whispering in her ear. I edged to the door, and saw Kennedy mouthing at me as I went,

"*Arnault...*" Silently her lips formed the word. "Fetch Arnault!"

I ran quickly up the stairs to Arnault's chamber, and blurted out, "In the Queen's apartments – Margaret Lindsay in a kind of seizure. Babbling about me, and of escape for the Queen!"

"Ah, Dieu!" With a sigh of resignation, Arnault heaved his bulk upright, grabbed a box that held some potions and pills, then hurried from the room. I paced about after he had gone, my mind a blank except for one thought. Margaret Lindsay's clinging devotion to the Queen threatened more of danger than her spying had ever done!

Arnault came back at last, puffing from the exertion of climbing the stairs, and collapsed thankfully into his chair. "I have given her a soothing powder," he announced. "She will sleep now."

I faced him, nerves all a-jangle, and exploded, "Damn your soothing powders. You should have found out if she knows anything about me!"

"I did." Arnault gave me his usual sardonic grin. "The girl is given to humours and vapours of all kinds. Therefore, she has nightmares. Also, she has become abject in her love for the Queen. And she does not particularly like you. Therefore her nightmares take the form of your doing something dreadful that will steal the Queen away from her. That was all there was to her outburst, my young friend. I questioned her closely – as closely as any physician could; and I do assure you that was the whole reason for it. She knows nothing of your plan. Absolutely nothing."

Yet still, I thought, she had some *sense* of what I intended. And it was this sense – this sort of animal feeling of suspicion about me, that had surfaced so strangely in her dreaming mind. It was an eerie feeling to have about her. And then there was Ellen. How far had *she* been influenced by Margaret's ravings? And what danger might that spell, if the girl made some further outburst. I turned this over in my mind for a day or two, and then – very obliquely – I began probing Ellen on the subject. But there, of course, I had reckoned without Ellen's usual bluntness of speech.

"Just stop beating around the bush," she told me; "and answer directly. *Are* you mixed up in some escape plan for the Queen?"

I put on my best air of injured innocence, and countered, "What on earth makes you ask that? You are not having nightmares too, are you?"

Ellen laughed. "I sleep soundly. I always have."

"And Margaret Lindsay is like her father – not violent, as he is; but crazy all the same. And so why ask such a question?"

"Because," Ellen said blandly, "I saw you once with a packet of letters. It was in the Queen's apartments. And you did not know I was there, in the inner chamber. I knew it was letters you had, too, because you dropped the packet in your haste to hide it inside your doublet. And that was when I had a good look at it."

My mind was racing as she spoke, darting here and there in search of a way out. I managed a laugh when she finished, and told her.

"You have caught me, Ellen – or rather, you have caught George. They were his letters – ones he had written to the Queen. I promised I would steal them back for him. It was just before he was banished, and he was afraid they would be found and – and compromise her."

Ellen took the bait in that word "compromise". Rising swiftly to it as a trout to a hatch of mayfly, she challenged, "Why? Were they love letters?"

"I am sorry, Ellen." Regretfully I shook my head. "I promised I would not say."

"They were! They *were* love letters!" Ellen's voice rose to a squeal of delight. Then she sighed a long, quivering sigh. "Oh-h-h, Will, is it not romantic? To be in love – and in love with the Queen!"

"I never said he was," I reminded her.

"No – but I guessed that for myself long before he *was* banished. And I must have been right, if he thinks his letters would compromise her. And listen, Will – " Ellen drew closer, a light of conspiracy in her eyes. Her delight in my story, I guessed, was about to lead her into some indiscretion of her own. And I was right! Her voice dropping to a whisper, she told me, "I can give you a secret, Will, in return for yours. The Queen *will* escape, just as she said to Moray she would. And she is planning it now. She told Margaret and me so, the day Margaret wept over her nightmare about you. But there will be no more of these nightmares now, because *she is going to take us both with her!*"

"Are you sure? But how could she manage that?" I was only playing for time with my questions; time to realise the Queen had taken the only way possible of making sure that poor, unhinged girl would no longer be a danger to her. But Ellen took me seriously enough – and also seemed to realise then, just how indiscreet she had been.

"Oh, there are ways," she said airily. "We talked

about them. But I am not stupid enough to repeat *that* part of the conversation."

And I would not be stupid enough to spoil the Queen's work by pressing her to say more! As for the alarm over the letters, that was safely over too, now that Ellen had so completely swallowed my story; and the more I allowed her to think she had some secret of her own to hide, the less likely she was to have fresh suspicions about mine. I made pretence of being crest-fallen, and said wistfully,

"As you please, Ellen. But I shall miss you when you *are* gone."

I had struck the right note there, it seemed – the one that pandered best to Ellen's vanity. She smiled kindly at me, vowed she would not forget me however far we might be separated by fortune; and left me, finally, looking the very picture of innocent smugness. I watched her go, thinking that Mistress Ellen was not nearly so shrewd as she imagined herself to be; and felt, like a tide rising in me, the exhilaration that comes from the knowledge of danger met head-on and thoroughly routed.

I was a different person then, it seemed to me, from everything I had been before. I was no longer just Will Douglas the page, the disregarded bastard of the house. I was Will Douglas, courier to the Queen of Scotland. I was the spymaster on whom she and all her friends depended, the one link between her and her gathering army. They could do nothing without me now; not one thing. What was more, the Queen had continued to show her gratitude with the gold she pressed on me every time I took her letters ashore to Beaton; so that suddenly also, I was rich! For the first time in my life I had money – real money, to save, to spend, just as I pleased. *Or* to gamble . . .

Now that, I told myself, would be a pleasure I had never imagined could be mine. To gamble with *gold* as my stake! The attraction of this thought began to pull me more strongly than anything I had ever felt before. And, I remembered, there were still two weeks to go before the 25th of March – plenty of time to have a few tastes of that pleasure. But cautious ones, of course.

I could not, for example, afford to draw attention on myself by lingering in the Kinross Inn. In the Castle guard-house, on the other hand, I had a few card-playing cronies who were used to seeing me produce such odd stakes as the silver buttons I had lost and won back again. A late-night game with them would do no harm . . .

I had more than one late-night game with my guard-house cronies – several, in fact; but I was still at my self-appointed post as usual, and still as alert as ever, when the day of the escape came at last. Mistress Lawson came ashore, dragging her right foot a little as she walked, the way she always did. But that was another of those small things I had noted and been careful to pass on. The Queen had practised that limping walk, and I was sure she would not forget to use it.

Mistress Lawson passed me by with her usual morning greeting. When she came back, I knew, she would nod to me before she tossed her bundle into the waiting boat. And the Queen would not forget, either, about that nod. I settled down to my pretence of inspecting all the Castle boats, and then turned in earnest to the inspection of my own little craft. The rowlocks needed some greasing. The boatman who had brought Mistress Lawson across watched me at this task, and called out eventually,

"You're busy, then."

I recognised him as one of the two men who had been waiting for hire on the night I had first brought Mistress Lawson to the Castle – one of the two who had joked with her on the Kinross side of the water. I gave him only a grunt in reply, not wanting to enter any conversation that would set his chaffing tongue at work on me. He got out of his boat and stamped around, calling out every now and then to the guards on the gate, the servant women who came to dip buckets of water out of the loch. His restlessness made *me* nervous, almost to the point of deserting my post to see if any hitch had occurred in my plan.

Then I saw her, the old washerwoman coming out through the Castle gate, head bent and shawl pulled forward, her bundle under her arm. The guards on the gate had not so much as glanced at her; and, I realised then, I could not myself tell whether it was the Queen or Mistress Lawson I was seeing. She limped the short distance from gate to landing-stage, gave her usual parting nod in my direction, and tossed her bundle into the boat. With the stiff movements natural to an old woman, she stepped aboard. The boatman pushed off from the landing-stage; and – if everything before that had gone according to plan – the Queen was on her way to freedom!

I straightened up from my own boat. From shore to shore the rowing time was between ten and twelve minutes, and I had Beaton's promise that she would be met on the mainland shore. In twelve minutes at the most, then, she would be riding towards her company of fifty – and I would be pushing out my own small boat to join them. As for the mount I would need, I could easily steal one from the stables of the New House!

Carried faintly across the water, I heard the sound of her boatman's voice. There was a laugh in the sound. Was he trying to joke with her, the way he had tried before to joke with Mistress Lawson? I saw him rest on his oars and lean towards the figure opposite him. One of his hands rose quickly to the shawl around her head. She jerked her head aside. Her arms flew up in the gesture of clutching the shawl more tightly around her. There was a swift flurry of water around the boat as the boatman began oaring it in a circle to turn it back towards our landing-stage.

I felt nothing at that moment – not despair, or disappointment, or anger; just nothing. The boatman had begun shouting, loud and hoarse, an alarm call to the guards on the gate. They came running to the landing-stage. The boatman looked back over his shoulder as he rowed. He was within thirty feet of the landing-stage now, and his call to the guards came with every word in it distinct.

"I have her! I have your prisoner!"

His boat bumped against the landing-stage. The shawled figure in it did not move; but the boatman was ashore on the instant, his voice coming out in a scared but triumphant babble.

"I teased her about keeping her shawl so close round her face. *"Come, mistress,"* I said, *"will you not let me see how pretty you are?"* Then I put up a hand to draw her shawl aside. She held it closer to her, and I saw her hands – so white, so soft. *"Those are a lady's hands!"* I said; and I pulled the shawl aside. And there she was – the Queen! *The Queen!"*

I moved towards the boat, forestalling the action

of the guards. The shawled figure raised her head to look up at me. Her face was deathly pale. Her eyes held a despair so profound that no words could have spoken it. She took the hand I held out to her. I helped her ashore; and then, with the guards following at our heels, I led her back into captivity.

14

I had a dog once of the kind known as a "licker". If he had a wound or sore of any kind, he would not only lick it clean, he would continue to lick and lick until the place was irritated beyond any chance of natural healing. And so it was with me after Sir William learned of the escape attempt.

The investigation he made then was thorough. His decisions were swift. Mistress Lawson, he declared, had been simply a dupe, and would be adequately punished by her loss of employment. But my case was different! *My* punishment would be a whipping, followed by banishment from the Castle – and that immediately, with no more than the clothes I wore and not even the chance of saying good-bye to Minny.

I had not the spirit left even to try seeking Minny out when the whipping was finished. I shrugged my doublet over my smarting shoulders, turned my back on the only home I had ever known, and rowed off in my little boat – but not to the mainland, where I might have had to face John Beaton or George Douglas. I made, instead, for another of the islands on the loch; the very small one known as Scart Island, where there was nothing except the remains of what had once been a fisherman's cottage. And there, among the fallen and crumbled stone of this ruin, I lay and licked at my wounds.

It was not that I blamed myself for the failure of the escape, because that, after all, had been due to nothing more than bad luck. But in spite of that, I knew, I still had to bear the blame of two serious faults committed *before* the escape. I had under-estimated my half-sister, Ellen. And when I had had my fling at gambling with gold, I had not taken suf-ficient account of Drysdale's hatred of the Queen.

My innocent-seeming Ellen had not been so inno-cent after all – as I learned to my cost when she hurried to tell Sir William of the letters she had seen me handling and when she boasted then, also, that she had not believed the lies I had told about them! As for Drysdale, he had heard whispers of my gambling in the guard-house. And, as he had argued in the testimony he also had hastened to give, where could such as I have got gold *except* from the Queen?

Then there had been mad Margaret's story of her dream about the great black bird. That had made a great impression – on the Old Lady, even more than on Sir William. And I had not been to blame, either, for Margaret's wild imaginings. But what did that matter now? Her story had most effectively put the final nail in my coffin – and oh, my God, how I wished they *had* killed me; put me altogether out of my misery instead of just banishing me to writhe in lonely self-contempt on that deserted island!

I had had my chance to help the Queen, and I had let myself be found out in that. Now *she* was alone, the contact with the mainland broken, no other ally in the Castle able to renew it. And all through *my* carelessness, *my* folly. That was the wound I licked at, and licked again, lying with my face in the wet grass between the stones, clawing at the stones themselves till my nails broke and my fingertips bled, and I sat up at last wondering aloud just why I should be suffering such pain.

The reason came slowly to me. I was just over a month short of my seventeenth birthday, and I had never before felt the pangs of love. But gradually as I sat there despising myself, remembering her, and wondering at the root of a pain so intense, I began to realise why I could not pick myself up from this experience and go on as jauntily as I always had before.

I was in love with her. I, Will Douglas, fortuneless, homeless, disgraced, was in love with the Queen; so in love, I would have died for her. And I wanted to die. Indeed, if shame could have killed, I would have died there and then, on Scart Island.

I began to weep. I had not wept since I was twelve years old, on the day I had fought a lad much bigger than myself to a standstill for jeering "bastard" at me; but I wept then till I was exhausted, and fell asleep where I lay. Cold woke me. I had left the Castle with no more than the clothes on my back, and they were rimed now with the frost of late March. I got to my feet and wandered aimlessly around the small confines of the island.

I could see the Castle from there. And so long as *she* was in the Castle, I thought, I could not bear to be out of sight of it. Without any idea beyond this I began to set up a sort of camp for myself, rebuilding the stone of the ruined cottage till it gave me a certain amount of shelter, gathering twigs to start a fire. I had the fishing tackle I kept always in my boat; and with that, I reckoned, I could supply myself with trout from the loch. I could go into Kinross, too, to buy oatmeal and salt – but not till I could depend on that gallant company of fifty being scattered back to their homes. Not till I thought Beaton and George would have ceased to look out for me as the rascal who had put paid to all *their* plans for the Queen.

There was only one way, I had found, to deal with the dog that was a "licker": That had been to cut the bottom out of a bucket, and then to invert the thing over his head so that it sat around his neck like a funnel-shaped collar projecting well beyond the tip of his muzzle. He could sleep, eat, and drink, while he wore this collar. He could do anything he normally did, in fact – except for licking his wound. Every time he tried that, he found the rigid frame of the bucket making a barrier between his tongue and the sore place. And the life – if it could be called a life – I had begun to invent for myself on Scart Island, would serve the same function for me, I thought, as the bucket had done for the dog.

I kept my fire going with driftwood, and sat for hours beside it fashioning rabbit-snares from strong sticks and bits of my fishing line. I fished for whole days at a time, sometimes from the shore of the island, sometimes drifting in my boat. I made catapults from wood and rabbit skin, and shot at seagulls bobbing on the waves close inshore. I raked over the ruins of the cottage for bits and pieces of pottery, and found also a rusty cooking-pot that I scoured with sand until this, too, became of use to me. I let a full week pass like this, however, before I dared to go into Kinross for oatmeal and salt. But no-one, it seemed, noticed me there; and so every now and then after that I made further trips to renew my supplies, going quickly into the village, buying furtively, and returning as quickly to my hiding-hole on Scart Island.

My life was firmly set then, in its new pattern. But there was still one terrible flaw in the reasoning that had led me to create it. I could keep my hands always busy. But I could not control my eyes. They were still always on the Castle, and on my distant view of Kinross; still always watching for the kind of movement that might be a sign of rescue or escape for her. And then there were the nights. I could not sleep, and yet neither could I work at night. The nights were when I was free to lick my wound till it bled again.

I began going into Kinross after dark, instead of in the daytime; heading always for some drinking-den or other, and always choosing those lying well away from the Kinross Inn. I still had some of the Queen's gold left, and so I had every chance of getting drunk in these places. And that was all I wanted then – to get so drunk that my mind would stop working, and the pain would go away. And some of the loneliness too, perhaps. But there was one night when I did go to the Kinross Inn. I was looking for Muriel; for her black eyes, the enticement of her smile. That was what I told myself, but in my heart I knew it was not these attractions that had drawn me there. It was simply that damnable loneliness, and the knowledge that there was no-one I *could* speak to now, except Muriel.

She was not there. I waited in the shadows outside the place till I saw the pot-boy come sauntering out, and asked him to take her a message from me. He looked me up and down, at my wrinkled clothes, my unkempt hair, and sneered,

"She'll not want to hear from the likes of you. Not where she is now, at any rate."

"Where? Where is she? Has she left the Inn?"

"More than three weeks ago. Gone to work at the New House, she has. Kirsty Thomson – her that used to be maid to Lady Margaret Douglas – she left to get married." A snicker of laughter, and then, "Not before time, if you ask me, seeing how round her belly was! And Mistress Muriel has got her place."

So there was not even a hope of seeing her again! I turned blindly away towards the outskirts of the village and one of the drinking-dens I knew I would find there. All the things I might have said to Muriel went through my mind as I headed to it. And Muriel, I told myself, would have understood. Girls always did understand, did they not, about being in love? But who was there to talk to now?

I reached the place – a dark, dirty, malodorous hole, it was – and started drinking. I spoke to no-one, and gradually all the faces around me began to blur in my sight. I was reaching the stage where I could stop thinking, stop feeling. My head began to droop. I felt a great desire to let it sink down altogether and to let myself sprawl with arms outstretched over the table. I swayed forward, and was in the very act of collapsing into this position, when a hand gripped the back of my neck and roughly jerked me back to the upright.

Mouth slack, eyes wildly squinting, I tried to see who had hold of me. The stool I sat on was kicked away. The hand on my neck took all my weight for a moment, then was joined by another hand gripping my shoulder. I mumbled protests, but the owner of the hands was merciless. He pushed me ahead of him to the door, then out into the yard. A man stood in my path there, a bucket of water in his hand. The man behind me said sharply,

"Douse him!"

The man with the bucket tipped its contents over me. The man behind me did the same with another bucket of water. I staggered upright from the second impact, wiped water from my face and eyes, and saw George Douglas and John Beaton standing watching me. Beaton put down his bucket the moment he saw I could stand of my own accord, and walked rapidly away. George held his ground, and asked,

"Can you walk?"

I shook more water from me, and questioned in my turn. "How did you find me?"

"The pot-boy. He is one of a number we paid to report any sight of you. Now, can you walk?"

"What's that to you?"

"Look," George told me grimly, "I risk my neck standing here talking to you. But I do it because I need you. *We* need you."

"I failed." Low and sullen, the words came from me. "I am of no more use to you."

"Yes, you are. Because we *must* have an ally inside the Castle. *And I can get you back there.* Now, if you are willing to take this last chance to help the Queen, will you walk with me to the New House?"

I found myself walking by his side, without any decision made, my mind still fuzzy with all I had drunk; and on our way to the New House, I listened as best I could to what he had to say.

"I have had secret meetings with my sisters," he told me; "and you know the tender feelings they have always had for you. Also, from the occasional sightings there have been of you in Kinross, I knew you still to be in the vicinity. And so I put it to the

157

Porches that remorse for your involvement in the escape attempt was the feeling that had held you here. They, in their turn, discovered for me that Sir William – believe it or not – has been pining for you. He is fonder of you than anyone supposed, it seems! And of course, he feels sorely bereft of all the services you used to give."

Guilt stabbed suddenly through the dullness of my mind, but George was still talking, telling me how he had persuaded the Porches to work on the affection Sir William still seemed to have for me.

"And the upshot of all this manoeuvring," George finished, "is that my brother is now willing to have you back in the Castle with him."

I could not speak for a time, I was so overcome by this news; and George let me be until I finally managed to ask, "Is it – is all this because you have some other form of escape planned?"

"We will talk of that," George said, "once the Porches have seen that you are bathed and fed and given some decent clothes."

We were at the stables of the New House by then. Just behind the stables lay the back entrance to the house itself. George stopped in the shadow of the stables, and asked, "*Are* you willing to go back, Will?"

Again I found I could not speak at first, but I did at last bring out a mutter of assent. "Then come to Beaton's room at the Inn tomorrow night at nine," he told me. "And Will – " He hesitated a moment, as if wondering how to put what he had to say next, then reached out a hand to me and finished, "Welcome back to our ranks!"

Our hands met in a long grip, but when he withdrew his at last, I still hung back from going to the door of the New House. I was not only soaked to the skin, after all. I had lived for five weeks in solitude and half-starvation, wearing the same clothes all that time, and drunk for part of it. I was ragged, filthy, more of a stinking scarecrow than a human being. What would those gentle ladies in the New House *say* if I walked in there? George read my mind.

"Go in, Will," he urged. "I have prepared them for what they will see. And they still want you to come to them."

I nodded, took my courage in both hands, and went up to the door of the New House. It yielded under my hand, and I stepped into the light and warmth the Porches had waiting for me.

15

I was prompt, the following night, in keeping my rendezvous at the Kinross Inn; but entering Beaton's room, I found, was no longer a simple matter of calling my name through the keyhole. Two burly young men stood outside his door, both armed cap-a-pie; and they held me there at sword-point until Beaton appeared to identify me in person.

I followed him back into his room, feeling shaken by this experience; and found George there also, along with two other men. One of these was a youngish fellow, with a great air of worldly experience about him. The other – a soldierly-looking man with curly grey hair – I guessed to be in his fifties. George made the introductions. The younger of the two was John Sempil, husband to one of the Queen's former ladies-in-waiting. The older man, I was somewhat awed to learn, was no less a person than her old friend, Lord Seton. Both of them looked me up and down with some wonder in their eyes.

The Porches had done their best, of course, to make me presentable again; but even a bath, a good meal, and decent clothing, had not been enough to give me back my normal appearance. For a start, I knew, I had lost so much flesh that my clothes were loose on me and my face had become gaunt. But what I did not realise was how my expression had altered. John Sempil looked from me to George, and said,

"I thought you said this was a merry fellow!"

"So I did," George agreed. "And he was – as I have always known him."

"Then, by God, he has changed," Sempil exclaimed, "I would not care to meet *him* in a dark alley, if he had some grudge against me!"

Lord Seton said brusquely, "Enough! If he can act the part of his former self, that is all we need."

I looked at George to see if he knew what was meant by that. George said quietly, "Will, you asked if we had another escape attempt in mind. And we have. One, this time, that *must* succeed. One that *must* have you there in the Castle."

I looked away and said in a flat voice. "I told you. I have had my chance."

"Listen, Will." George took me by the shoulders, so that I was forced to meet his eyes again. "The time has never been more ripe for the Queen's escape. All her supporters are ready and waiting for her. We are still managing to hold that fox, Argyll, to the promise that will give us superior numbers. And if we do not take advantage of that *now*, the chance of victory for her may be gone forever."

They were all intently watching me. I looked aside again, biting my lip, saying nothing. George gave my shoulders a little shake. "If I explain to these others what I have in mind," he persisted, "will you tell us then whether or not you will do as I ask?"

Still I had nothing to say; but George had apparently decided now to take my silence for consent to proceed. He turned from me, took pen and paper from Beaton's desk, and rapidly sketched the main features of the Castle. The others looked over his shoulder as he worked, with both Sempil and Lord Seton occasionally throwing curious glances at me.

"There!" George sat back at last, and began demonstrating from his sketch. "There we have the gate in the courtyard wall. There also, on the second floor of the main tower, is the Great Hall with the screen that runs across the greater part of its width. This spiral stair in the Hall's south-eastern corner leads up to the Queen's apartments on the floor above. There is no way she can leave the tower, therefore, except by coming down that stair, slipping past this gap between the end of the screen and the south wall of the Hall, then using the protection of the screen to gain the doorway of the Hall. From that point she must proceed down the outer stair that leads to the courtyard. And there is no way she can leave the courtyard itself, except by that gate in the wall."

Sempil leaned forward to put his finger on the sketch. "That spiral stair," he said, "must go down to the area below the Hall as well as leading to the apartments above it. What lies below?"

"The kitchen," George told him. "And of course, the kitchen also has a doorway into the courtyard. But to leave the tower by *that* door would mean passing through a whole horde of servants there – not to mention the guards who come to the kitchen for meals and gossip in their off-duty times."

Lord Seton said, "And I suppose you have ruled out the possibility of escape through a window of her apartments?"

"Yes, indeed, my lord." George tapped the plan

decisively. "All her windows are under observation from one angle or another. Besides which, she would risk injury in the descent from so high a point; and the boy could not carry her out."

I had heard enough by then. George was doing no more than repeating all the points we had so often discussed before. And he had still said nothing to solve the final problem of getting her through that gate in the courtyard wall. Curtly I told him, "You are wasting your time with all this. I cannot get her out at all."

"Oh yes, you can!" George looked up at me, smiling a little. "If you do as I say, she can walk out of the Castle any time you choose."

"Past the guards on her door?" Resentfully I returned his look. "Past those on the gate? I tried that – remember? And you know how long it took to arrange."

"Ah yes. And time is of the essence now. But, Will – " George's smile was growing wider. "Just think of the *pattern* of the guards' duties. You are as familiar with that – are you not? – as I am."

I was, of course. And the pattern never varied. At seven o'clock every evening when Sir William locked the gate in the courtyard wall, the guards who had been on duty there stood down for the night. And so did those on the Queen's door. Why should they not, after all? The doorway of the Great Hall *was* the only way the Queen could get out of the tower and into the courtyard. The gate in the wall *was* the only way out of the courtyard itself. And the moment Sir William sat down to supper after he had locked the gate, he put the key –

"The key . . .!" I did no more than breathe the words, but George heard them.

"Yes, Will, the key to the gate!" He nodded to me, his smile broadening to a grin of conspiracy that took in the others also. "Because, you see," he explained to them, "the guards on the Queen's door and those on the courtyard gate are dismissed from duty once that gate is locked for the night. And so, if the boy waits till after it *is* locked, and then steals the key, he rids himself of the whole problem of smuggling the Queen past those guards."

"Of course, of course!" Eagerly Lord Seton agreed. "He simply unlocks the gate again, lets the Queen through – "

"And rows her ashore," George finished triumphantly, "in his own little boat."

I began to laugh, weakly, foolishly. It was such a simple idea; so brilliantly simple! How had George come to think of it? And why had *I* never thought of it before? I could visualise exactly, too, the situation that would make it possible for me to steal the key; and already, in my mind's eye, I could see that happening. George rose and came towards me, asking,

"Can you do it? *Will* you do it?"

I nodded, still laughing. Lord Seton frowned at this, and said sharply, "Steady yourself, boy, and give us a proper answer."

Suddenly then, through the foolish sound I was making, I heard again my own agonised weeping on Scart Island. Behind all the faces watching me, I saw *her* face. And it was not the sharpness of Lord Seton's voice that steadied me enough to answer,

"Yes, my lord. I will do it."

Seton eyed me in silence for a moment; then, abruptly, he asked, "And you do understand the risk you will be running this time?"

Did he think I was afraid? I faced squarely up to

him, and said with all the force I could muster, "I told you, my lord, I would do it. And I will, supposing I were to be hanged tomorrow for it."

A look of grim triumph spread over Lord Seton's features. Quietly, from behind me, John Beaton said, "I told you once you had the makings of a spymaster in you. But I think now – " He paused, and I turned to see him looking around the other three. "I think now," he went on, "I can speak for us all when I say that you have also the makings of a brave man."

There was a general murmur of assent, to which Lord Seton added, "But you do realise how quickly you will have to work?"

"Yes," I told him. "But it is still up to you, my lord, to tell me exactly what time I do have."

"My lord," George interposed, "the boy can return tomorrow – Friday – to the Castle. That will bring us to April 30th."

"And we could be completely ready three days from now – by May 2nd." Lord Seton muttered this half to himself. "If we could have her out by that date..."

May 2nd – that was my birthday. George began speaking, and I brushed this thought aside to listen to him. "If you will permit us to explain to the boy, my lord," he suggested, and then turned from Lord Seton to me.

"Once you *are* back in the Castle," he told me, "what we plan is this. I will divert suspicion of our intentions by sending word to the Old Lady that I mean to leave the country for good, to seek my fortune in France. And on the day before the escape, I shall appear openly at the New House under pretext of saying good-bye to her."

He paused then to look at Beaton, who immediately added to this, "And on the day of the escape itself, I shall also appear openly in Kinross with a bodyguard of ten men to escort Mr Douglas on his supposed journey to take ship for France. But those ten men, of course, will be the Queen's immediate escort when she touches at the mainland."

"Of which escort," Sempil chimed in, "I shall be one. And the moment we have her among us, we will ride to rendezvous with Lord Seton's company."

"Fifty of them," Lord Seton himself finished, "waiting in a hollow on Benarty Hill, from whence we can directly observe Her Grace's journey ashore."

They had it all so well planned this time! And yet, once I *did* have that key in my possession, I still could not get her out of the tower without the risk of Sir William seeing her as she passed by the gap at the limit of the Great Hall's service screen. How could I plan for that? And in so short a time, too? Friday, Saturday, Sunday; and they wanted me to get her out *on* the Sunday.

Sunday, May the 2nd... The date rang again in my head, with the emphasis this time on the word "Sunday", and the feeling also that there was something I ought to have remembered, apart from the 2nd of May being my birthday. *Sunday*, May the – I had it! The first Sunday in May was always a holiday. And I could make good use of that holiday coinciding, this year, with my birthday. Very good use! I turned to Lord Seton, and told him,

"I can have her out on Sunday, my lord."

There was a moment's silence, and then a loud sigh of relief from all four men. I addressed them generally. "But you will have to bear in mind that there is only one circumstance in which I can steal the key. And because of that, I must be sure the escort will meet my boat no later than a quarter after seven o'clock on that evening."

"At the landing-stage for the New House," George said quickly. "Can you bring her in there?"

I hesitated to answer this. From our own west landing-stage to the landing-stage of the New House would certainly be my shortest crossing. But Sir William had that particular crossing directly under observation from the west window of the Great Hall – and at the very time, too, when I would have to make it. Cautiously, I asked,

"Why the New House?"

"Because I will have to be quickly informed of the moment to bring up my reinforcements," Lord Seton told me. "And the very fact that my hiding-place overlooks the crossing to the New House means that the Queen herself could wave the signal I will need."

"And a further good reason," George added, "is that the horses in the New House stables are the *only* ones immediately available for pursuit. But we mean to foil that pursuit by stealing those horses to make mounts for our own men."

I thought of the time when *I* had planned to steal a mount for myself from the New House stables. But stealing all of Sir William's horses was a bold as well as a cunning stroke! As for the signal to Lord Seton, there was no doubt that one given by the Queen herself would be the speediest way to send news of her approach. I would think of that west window, I decided; and I would find some method of dealing with Sir William's view from it. I glanced from George to Lord Seton, and said,

"Very well, my lord. I will bring Her Grace in at

the New House. And I will ask her to wave a scarf or some other such thing as soon as I think we are far enough from the island for her to do so safely."

"Good!" Lord Seton rose briskly on the word, and glanced around the other three. "So is it all settled now?"

Beaton said quickly, "Except for one thing, my lord." His glance flickered between George and myself; and the glance was followed by a silence – a silence, I began to realise, which held a certain awkwardness. George spoke, without looking directly at me.

"Er – Will, I – um – I said enough earlier to let you understand that this is the one attempt that *must not* fail. And you remember the pearl the Queen gave me to be returned as the signal for that? Well, she must have it back now. But not by your hand, because – "
He paused, flushing in embarrassment; and it was then that the reason for the feeling of that silent moment dawned on me.

She had to be as much convinced as they were of the urgency of this attempt. But I was "the merry fellow", the fool who had let myself be outwitted by a little girl like Ellen, the boaster who had swaggered under the spying eyes of Captain Drysdale. If the signal of the pearl came now from me, she might not – probably would not – take it seriously enough.

" – because of the reputation you have got for yourself," George continued awkwardly. "And so I will have to find some other way of sending it to her."

I had swallowed my medicine by then, bitter though the taste of it had been. I could even see the answer to George's dilemma; and, ironically enough, I thought, it was my own scrapegrace ways that had provided it.

"Muriel!" I uttered the one word of my answer aloud; and then, as George frowned in puzzlement at me, I repeated, "Muriel – Muriel Matheson, daughter to the innkeeper here. She is maid to the Old Lady now. And Muriel will do anything you ask of her, if she knows it is to be done for me. Give *her* the pearl when you go on Saturday to say good-bye to the Old Lady. And then, when she attends the Old Lady on the daily visit to the Castle, she can give it to the Queen."

"H'mm." George considered this, and then said, "This girl – Muriel – would have to spin some tale to account for the Queen's jewel being in *her* possession."

He looked expectantly at me; and so did the other three. *Waiting for the accomplished liar to speak . . .* I said impatiently,

"Well, that is easy enough. Tell her to say she got it from the boatman who discovered the Queen in her guise as the washerwoman. The earring fell off that day when he so roughly pulled her shawl aside. But he has only just found it, and given it to Muriel to be returned to the Queen."

Lord Seton asked, "Could the girl keep her face straight, telling such a tale?"

"Muriel?" I glanced at him, and laughed. "I know her, my lord; and she is a born deceiver! Besides, I can brief her on what she has to do. I will find some chance for that before I leave the New House tomorrow."

"In that case . . ." Lord Seton sketched a bow in the direction of George and John Beaton, motioned Sempil to come with him, and then held out his hand to me. "The next time I see you," he said, "I hope it will be in the presence of Her Grace. And with God's help, boy, I think you will make that possible."

The grasp of his hand in mine was firm, dry, and warm. The thought, *"I could trust such a hand"* flashed across my mind. Then he was gone, with Sempil following, and George telling me,

"And now, Will, I had better see *you* on your way."

We walked together out of the Inn, and there was nothing then to stop me taking my leave of him; yet still I lingered. My head was full of the plan that had come to me in outline, back there in Beaton's room; and the plan linked up so neatly with something I had once said to George that I could not help asking him,

"George, do you remember how you reproached me, once, for playing the fool? And do you remember what I said to you when you told me then, that clowning would not help the Queen?"

Frowningly, George strove to recollect our onetime conversation, and managed at last, "You said something like – *'the most dangerous of situations can be disguised in laughter'*."

"That was exactly what I said." I grinned at him, with the impulse that had prompted the remark bubbling up again inside me. "But I finished then by telling you also that the Queen might yet have need of a Court jester."

"Ye-e-e-s," George agreed cautiously. "I believe you did. And so?"

"And so," I told him, "I plan for Sunday to prove me right in that. And believe me, George, if only I can jest enough on that day – and jest in sufficient earnest, too – there is no doubt we *will* have our Queen again."

16

I took a loving leave of the Porches next morning –
but not before I had spoken secretly to Muriel and
got her consent to do what George would ask of her
on the day following. Being a lady's maid suited her,
I thought. She looked more charming than ever in
the frilled cap and velvet-bodiced gown the Old
Lady had provided. She flashed her coquettish smile
at me when I told her so; and for old times' sake,
then, I sealed our bargain with the kiss she expected
of me.

The Old Lady saw me before I was too far away
from her room and made a guess at where I had been.
She knew what Muriel was like by then, I suppose,
and she certainly thought she knew me! She had to
hide a smile all the same, I noticed, before she said,

"So you are already up to your old tricks, are
you?"

I grinned at her with all my former impudence,
and said, "Maybe, Your Ladyship. But you are too
beautiful still, are you not, to be jealous of a little
lady's maid?"

The smile came out of hiding then, and finished in
a shout of laughter. "We've missed you, you fool,"
she told me, gave me a token box on the ear, and

went on her way still chuckling.

And that was how it would be for the next three days, I vowed. I would show a properly humble gratitude for my reinstatement, of course, but I would still go on being the Will Douglas they were all expecting to meet again – as impudent as before, as much of a fool as I had ever been. I would play a role, in effect; the role of my former self. And if I could not succeed in that role, then I was not the actor I had always supposed myself to be!

I made straight for Sir William's apartments when I got to the Castle, and was brought up short there by the sight of Lady Agnes lying in bed with a new-born infant in her arms.

"Will!" She smiled her usual vague smile up at me. "You're back. Then you can take the baby from me a moment, if you please."

I took a gingerly hold of the baby while she prepared to heave herself out of bed; and then stood noting the accumulation of Sir William's personal gear lying around. They needed a nurse for him too, not a page, I thought; and the moment Lady Agnes took the child back from me, I set about putting things back to the order I had always kept for them. Lady Agnes prattled on while I worked, proud of being so quickly on her feet again after the birth, proud that this would enable her to resume her duties with the Queen.

But that will not stop *me*, Your Ladyship, I told her silently; and let her chatter flow over me while I thought ahead to the details of my plan. My time was so short. And there were so many of these details to be worked out! A nurse came bustling in to relieve Lady Agnes of the baby while she retired to dress herself, and minutes after the nurse came Sir

William. He looked me up and down, unsmiling, his face closed to any welcome. I knelt to him, kissed his hand, and said humbly,

"I thank you, sir, for your forgiveness, which is more than I deserve of you."

"Er – well, I thought – Since you are young, and foolish by nature... And – er – if you promise never to repeat your fault..."

Sir William was stuttering as he always did when he was embarrassed; and that, I thought, was the chance to have the ball in my court. I looked up at him and said with pretended fervour, "Of course I promise, sir. And sir, you *are* glad to have me back – are you not?"

"Certainly. Certainly I am." Sir William flushed a little, and at last began to smile. "I – er – I have missed you badly, boy."

"Then, sir, we must celebrate!" I jumped to my feet with the words, and rushed cheerfully on, "You are glad to have me back, I am glad to be here, and – have you forgotten, sir? – Sunday is my birthday. And Sunday is also a holiday. We could have a whole day's celebration then!"

"Oh, Will!" Lady Agnes had reappeared in time to hear this, and she stood looking now in dismay at me. "But I am just out of my confinement, and a whole day's celebration would mean all sorts of preparations. The food, the wine – there would be so much to do!"

"But *you* would not need to do it." Pleading, I held out my hands to her. "We could hire Mistress Matheson to bring over all we need from the Kinross Inn."

"And who would pay for that?" Sir William enquired – but not too sternly, I thought. I flashed a grin at him, and said, "*You* might, sir. As a birthday present for me, perhaps?"

Sir William chuckled then, as I had hoped he would. "You have not changed," he said. "My God, you have not changed one little bit!"

"Oh, but I will, I will," I told him, and cut a clown's caper that made him chuckle all the more. "Once I am seventeen on Sunday, I promise I will be the most sober fellow alive. If *you* will promise to let me have this one last fling with my celebration."

"I will think about it," Sir William conceded. "But meanwhile, my lad, it is back to duty for you. And the first of your duties, remember, is to attend on *me*."

Briefly then, he kissed Lady Agnes, made a casual show of admiring the baby, and beckoned me to follow him from the apartment. I kept at his heels as he went downstairs, and stopped when he did, outside the Queen's apartments. He turned to look back at me then, his face once more severe.

"I wish to let Her Grace also see the extent of my forgiveness," he told me, "therefore you will attend me even in here. But remember your promise, and – I warn you – do not try again to take advantage of me."

Now was the time for another touch of humble gratitude. "I would not dream of doing so, sir," I protested, "unless it were to tell Her Grace, even before you do, how gracious you have been to me."

Sir William gave a satisfied nod, then knocked at the door. I entered the room a pace or two behind him, and once more found myself in the presence of the Queen. She was newly dressed, sitting before her mirror with her hair still loose about her shoulders. Her eyes met mine through a fine, floating veil of its

174

gleaming strands, and I felt the tingling pleasure of that encounter in a flush that seemed to run from my hairline to my heels. Sir William's bow and his opening words gave me a few seconds to recover myself; but I was still feeling the effect of that flush when she answered,

"Yes, indeed, Sir William. I do see how forgiving you have been. And how kind to me too, to let me enjoy again the company of my little orphan."

Sir William laughed. "Not so little now, Your Grace. He will be seventeen on Sunday."

I seized on the chance he had given me, and said quickly, "And I am so pleased to be back, Your Grace, that I mean my birthday celebration to make Sunday a holiday to remember. If – " I hesitated, glancing at Sir William. "If I am allowed to, that is."

"But of course you must be allowed!" Reproach in her voice, the Queen followed my glance. "Why should he not, Sir William?"

Sir William shrugged, and did everything he could to avoid meeting the Queen's gaze. But I kept my eyes hard on her, and had the satisfaction of seeing her become aware of the intensity of my look. "Lady Agnes," Sir William was saying lamely. "She is just out of her confinement, you understand. And all the preparations that would be involved – she could not undertake that. It would mean hiring from the Kinross Inn – a costly business; and – " His eyes finally settled on me. "And I have not yet decided whether he is worth all that."

"Then I shall decide for you." Smiling, the Queen rose and went to her desk, lifted its lid, and called, "Will, come here to me."

I went towards her and stood by the desk, with one hand resting on its edge. She saw the tiny wedge of paper I let fall then, from my fingers into the desk itself, but did not blink an eye to betray her knowledge while she told me,

"I will give you this to pay for your celebration, Will, on condition I am invited to it. Now, does that please you?"

I looked from the roll of gold coins in her hand to Sir William, and said, "If it also pleases Sir William, Your Grace."

"Well, Sir William?" Smiling, she turned to him. "Does the boy have his celebration, or does he not?"

"Your Grace – " Sir William was flushed with embarrassment. "You are too generous! But if you insist on paying, then by all means I agree that the boy should have his way."

And now was the time to revert again to impudence! Quickly I chimed in, "In that case, sir, I will be as kind to you now as the Queen has been to me. I will choose from you a birthday present that will cost you nothing, because it is a gift that money cannot buy. I choose ... I choose..." I stopped, holding him in suspense till he finally demanded,

"What?"

"I can guess!" the Queen exclaimed. "Sunday is the day for May games; and because it is your birthday, you want the right to preside over them. You want Sir William to let you be the Lord of Misrule!"

"For that one whole day – yes, Your Grace, that *is* what I want." I turned from her to smile at Sir William. "If you will grant me that favour for my gift, sir?"

I had him in a position now where he knew he would sound churlish if he refused – especially so since he was already aware he had been made to seem mean over paying for the celebration itself. I won-

dered if the Queen would guess that my manoeuvring towards this point was connected with the
folded-small note I had dropped into her desk. I saw
her fingers stray towards it as Sir William hesitated
over his consent, and prayed she would wait till we
were gone before allowing those impatient fingers to
make any further move.

Sir William's doubting look began to turn into a
smile. He liked May games as much as anyone, after
all; and he had already admitted his pleasure in my
return. I stifled the long breath of relief I wanted to
draw when he finally voiced his consent; and gave
him, instead, the kind of fulsome thanks that flat-
tered him into a mood where he would have granted
almost anything I asked. But that, for the moment,
was all I wanted from him; and my next target – to be
reached as quickly as I could – was some method of
disabling every boat on the island, except my own.

"You spoke of duties," I reminded him once we
had left the Queen's apartments; "but who has been
looking after the boats while I was gone?"

"Captain Drysdale," he told me. "Not the most
suitable person, I agree. But who else was there?"

"Sir William – " I stopped in my tracks, so that he
had to halt too. "I was seduced from all duty to you, I
know. But I have repented, and these boats are important to us. I *must* make sure they are all still
sound."

"Then make sure, make sure." Amiably he waved
me off, and I sped down to the boats to work out the
best way of putting them temporarily out of action.
The loss of the key, I was well aware, could be discovered within seconds of my stealing it. But that
loss would have to be connected first to the fact that
I, too, was missing; and so I would have perhaps three

minutes in hand for the exercise of getting the Queen from her apartments to my boat. Any time after that, however, could see the pursuit started; and so I *had* to delay that pursuit by at least the further ten or twelve minutes I needed to row her to the mainland.

A hole in the bottom of each boat would have served my purpose, of course. But the boat-timbers were too sturdy to be easily and quickly holed. I could not damage them too soon before the actual moment of escape, either, since that would be to risk too-early a discovery of their condition. Something more subtle was called for . . .

I stood staring at the boats, and thinking. There was a rough westerly wind blowing – the kind we sometimes had to suffer for days at a time; and according to our usual practice then, the boats had been drawn up on shore at the sheltered east landing-stage. As usual, also, they were held there by a chain slotted through an iron ring fixed to the prow of each boat. And that chain, I realised, was my answer. One end of it was firmly stapled to a wooden bollard. The other end was coiled around a second bollard. And so long as that chain could not run freely through the rings on the prow of each boat, *none of them could be released*.

There was one way I could make sure of that! A wooden peg driven through each link in the loose end of the chain would be enough to prevent it running through those iron rings. And that exercise, I reckoned, was something I could complete in the very last quarter of an hour before the escape. But what were the chances of my being observed in this? There would be no danger from the guards on the gate, since that was set in the north wall of the court-yard. But what about windows? There was a big east window in the Queen's sitting-room; and Sir William would be there, serving supper to her, at the very time I would be working on the chain. Could I risk him seeing me then, from that east window?

I would have to, I decided. There was no way, after all, of avoiding that risk, any more than I could avoid all the others still to be faced. But I did at least have a plan for dealing with them as they arose! With a certain wry satisfaction in the way that plan was taking shape, I turned from the boats and went hurrying off to see Minny.

She had been expecting me, I realised, when I saw the expression on her face. But she had still not been expecting the changed expression *I* wore. The gladness of her look changed suddenly to pity; and without a word beyond her first cry of greeting, she rose to fold me in her arms. We stood thus together for a long moment before she let me go, and said quietly,

"You are going to try again. Is that it?"

"Yes. And this time, Minny, I am going to succeed. It is life or death now."

"Your death?"

"Certainly, if my plan goes wrong."

"Oh, Will – " Her lips quivered. "Whatever happens then, you will be going away again. But for good, this time."

I reached for her hands and pressed them between my own. "Only at first, Minny, because I must escape with her. But I will let you know where we have gone, and then you will join me. To live with me. To look after me. Will you do that?"

The tears that had threatened came freely then. "God knows you need looking after!"

"Mi-i-i-nny!" I gave her hands a gentle shake.

"There is no time to cry if you want to save my life. I want you to work for me – to work harder and quicker than you have ever done."

"Tell me, then." Minny wiped the tears away with the back of her hand, and faced me bravely. "But let me tell you one thing first, Will. You are – "

The brave front vanished. Her head drooped. The hands between my own trembled. I had to make it easier for her. I said gently. "I'm your son. No need to tell me. I have often felt it so – Minny."

She looked up at me, slowly. "And you – you do not blame me?"

"Now," I said, "you are just being foolish. And at this moment, Mistress Douglas, a foolish woman is no use to *me*."

She tried to answer the smile I was giving her, and – being Minny – she succeeded. "Now you are more like yourself," I told her; and as quickly as I could then, I outlined what she would have to do.

I wanted her, I told her, to make me two of the costumes worn by such of the soldiers' wives as were local women. Full skirts of black, tight bodices of scarlet, and high-crowned black hats – that was the kind of dress that distinguished these women. And any kind of distinctive dress, of course, is the best for disguise.

"Because then," I explained to Minny, "the on-looker assumed from that dress that he is seeing only the kind of person he *expects* to see wearing it."

"But why two?" Minny asked. "Why two, for God's sake?"

I hushed her down to launch into the next part of my tale – a vivid recollection coming to me as I spoke of the Queen walking in the garden with her maids, and Ellen remarking that Kennedy's lack of inches

180

made the three of them look like *"two women walking with a little girl."* But if the Queen were to try escaping alone, I reminded Minny, her unusual tallness would be the very feature that could betray her disguise. It was a common thing, on the other hand, to see one of the local women with a young daughter in a dress identical to her own. And so, if the Queen took Kennedy with her, their differing heights would be just what was needed to mislead people into the impression I wanted to create – that of a soldier's wife and child, walking hand in hand across the courtyard.

Minny began looking to the chests and cupboards that held all her spare bolts of cloth. "I have red flannel," she muttered. "I can manage the black, too. And I think I already have one of those hats around here somewhere." She rose towards one of the cupboards, and then turned to ask, "How long do I have to do all this?"

"Till Sunday afternoon."

"Your birthday – !

"Yes. I have persuaded Sir William to let me celebrate it with May revels that will take up the whole of that day. The Queen will be at the revels too; and in the middle of the afternoon, when her apartments are empty and therefore unguarded, you can slip into them to hide the costumes in the chest that lies to the left of her writing-desk."

"I had better get to work!" Minny threw open the cupboard door and began to rummage along the shelves, then turned to ask, "But Will, how will you let the Queen know what is expected of her?"

My mind slid back to the previous night in the New House and the writing of the note I had so recently dropped inside the Queen's desk. "No need to worry about that," I answered Minny. "I have already found a way of telling her."

"But will she do as you say? I mean – " Minny faced again to the shelves to hide her embarrassment. " – after the last time?"

I got to my feet and asked, "Can you promise to do your share, Minny?"

She threw a hurt look at me. "Do you need to ask that, Will?"

"Then trust me for the rest," I told her. "And come tomorrow, Minny, when the Queen receives a certain signal that will be sent to her then, you can rely on it that she will trust me also."

I do not think Minny would have argued any further on this but I could not have stayed, in any case, to find out. The morning was flying away from me. It would soon be time for me to serve Sir William's dinner, and I still had two other people to see. I decided on Arnault before dinner, and Diderot afterwards; and hurried off to Arnault's room. He looked up at me as I came in and said sarcastically,

"*Eh bien!* So we are once again honoured!" Sharply he closed the book he had been reading, and rushed on without giving me a chance for any word in reply. "And have you learned yet of how *we* persisted in our efforts to arrange the Queen's escape once you had paid the penalty of your folly? Do you know anything at all of the shifts and stratagems we had to contrive to keep in touch with the good young M'sieur Douglas and his helpers? But no! How could you be aware of that? And what do you care anyway, steeped in self-love as you are! But let me tell you this, young sir, let me warn you now – "

He was wound up to a high pitch, I realised; and so there was nothing for it but to let him ramble on till he had let out all the spleen and bitterness that seemed to have built up against me. I deserved it, after all, and he could not say anything I had not already said to myself. I waited with bent head until his voice tailed away into mutterings of disgust and despair. He had turned away from me by then, to slump forward over his desk. I touched his shoulder, ignoring the way he flinched from the feel of my hand, and quickly told him,

"I am not here to defend myself from the past, M'sieu Arnault, but to tell you of the future. At seven o'clock on Sunday evening, the Queen will be as free as a bird. That is a promise. But it is not one I can carry out unless *you* promise to help me at a crucial stage of her escape."

His head jerked up. His face turned in astonishment towards me. Rapidly and briefly I told him of the meeting in the Kinross Inn, the plan that had sprung then to my mind, and the part he would have to play in it. He listened without once taking his eyes off me, the surprise on his face changing to wonder, and then to delighted approval. To my great embarrassment then, he jumped to his feet, seized me by the shoulders, kissed me resoundingly on either cheek, and showered as many blessings on me as he had previously flung curses.

As quickly as I could, I freed myself from his embrace. It was past time, I reckoned, for the Queen's dinner to be served, which meant Sir William would soon be calling me to serve his own. And I could not so soon risk my welcome home by being late for that! With Arnault's voice still following me, I hurried out and dashed downstairs to the kitchen.

Diderot was there. I caught a glimpse of his big,

handsome face in the corner where he usually sat after he had finished his work on the Queen's dinner. I stood getting my breath back while the trays for the Great Hall were arranged, then placed myself as usual at the head of the service procession, and walked upstairs to the Hall to find a very jovial Sir William waiting for me to put his dish in front of him.

"Ah ha, Will!" He rubbed his hands. "Like old times, eh?"

"Just like old times, Sir William." But my hand was trembling as I poured his wine; and as the meal went on, I could have shouted with vexation at the way Lady Agnes toyed slowly with her food.

"To-morrow morning, Will," Sir William said between mouthfuls, "you can go over to the Inn and arrange what you want with Mistress Matheson. Eh?"

I was swallowing down my own dinner as fast as I could. I said, "Yes, sir. Thank you, sir." And turning to Lady Agnes he remarked complacently,

"You see, my dear – a reformed character!"

I rose quickly in my role of reformed character to supervise the clearing of the table, went soberly out of the Hall and back down to the kitchen. Diderot spoke only French, I knew; and so, with every step I took, I was rehearsing what I would say to him. "*Be brief*", I warned myself. That would be the best way to make my meaning absolutely clear to him.

Diderot was at the chopping-block, butchering the carcass of a sheep. He had a long and sharp boning-knife in his right hand. His cleaver – the cleaver Arnault had threatened he might use on *me* – lay within his reach. I had a moment's panic when I thought I could not remember the French word for "cleaver". Then I had it – *fendoir; le fendoir*.

I spoke low to him, ignoring the suspicion that looked out at first from his face. "Diderot, you know why I was banished. I am back for the same purpose. *But you must help.* At seven o'clock on Sunday, the Queen and one of her maids will come down the steps from the Great Hall. They must reach the gate without being stopped by any servant, or by any of the guards. And I want you to make sure of that. You understand?"

Diderot nodded. His eyes went to his cleaver. I said, "Yes, my friend. Come out from the kitchen at seven o'clock on Sunday night. I will meet you. Stand so that you can watch what happens in the courtyard while the Queen walks to the gate. And if anyone tries to lay hands on her – "

Diderot's face lifted quickly to the kitchen's smoky ceiling. Then he looked down again, the question about Sir William plain in his eyes. I shook my head, and said,

"No, not him, Diderot. Not with the cleaver, at least. And no woman with the cleaver, either. But with anyone else, my friend, you have a free hand."

Diderot reached out to exchange the knife for the cleaver, and with pudgy fingers caressing its heavy blade, he promised quietly, "*Personne ne me passera pas.*"

No, I thought; no-one *would* get past him. And now, in all the rest that remained to be done, the responsibility would be mine alone.

17

Sunday the 2nd of May dawned bright and clear, with the west wind still blowing but much moderated in force. I was out early, supervising the servants at setting up a long line of tables in the garden, and then secretly visiting Minny to see if she had the two costumes ready. She was still hard at work on them; but, she promised, she would have them finished on time. Ellen passed me on the stairs as I went in from hearing this, and said,

"*You* look cock-a-hoop today."

"And why not," I asked, "on my birthday?"

Ellen surveyed me again and pronounced her next verdict. "You have grown thinner."

I had not spoken directly to her since my return; and now, I guessed, she wanted to prolong the conversation. But I was too wary to be trapped again by Ellen! "And taller," I retorted; "*and* older. Which means I have no time now for little girls like you!"

I chucked her under the chin as I spoke, and carried on upstairs, laughing at the disgusted face she made. In my own room – a cupboard-sized hole in the wall two steps down from Sir William's door – I changed into my best clothes. Today, we would all be wearing our best. Either that, or those who felt like it would wear a masquerade costume. But the important thing for me in wearing my best was that it meant I could also wear my sword. I belted this on and went down to look out for the boats coming over with the wine and food from the Kinross Inn.

Mistress Matheson came with the first of these, talkative as always. I gave her instructions on laying out the provisions, and then went off to cut myself a straight stick of hazel to use as my wand when Sir William appointed me Lord of Misrule for that day. The tables were laid out with flagons of wine all along their length, when I got back with my stick. I groped in the bushes for another flagon I had hidden there – one I had chosen for its distinctive shape, and then filled with coloured water, and placed it also on the table. The Lord of Misrule, I intended to inform everyone, would not condescend to drink any but his own wine – and that a strong one, fit for such an occasion!

Ellen came dancing out into the garden, dressed in a gown of pale blue satin that gave her a look of almost ethereal beauty. Solid, sensible Ellen. Sly little Ellen! But she was so pretty now that I forgave her. Margaret Lindsay trailed behind her, looking wan in some sort of dull green. But Margaret, I thought, would have looked wan, whatever colour she wore. I gave them both some wine, and drank so heartily myself that Ellen exclaimed,

"You will be drunk before dinner-time!"

"Certainly," I told her. "And I shall be drunk after dinner-time too."

"Then you will be a fit Lord of Misrule," Sir William's voice said from behind me.

I looked around and saw that the garden had begun

to fill up with family and servants. Muriel was there, trailing behind the Old Lady with a cloak and a pile of cushions in her arms. I raised my eyebrows in question to her, and she answered with a long, slow wink that I hoped was intended to assure me of the safe delivery of the pearl. The Porches came swirling round me, each of them with her attendant admirer – except for Lady Lindsay, who was now arm-in-arm with Margaret. Diderot strode up to the tables, proudly carrying a huge dish piled with fruit made out of marzipan. His personal gift to the Queen, I guessed. Diderot prided himself on his skill in such confections. But where was the Queen herself? The sun was high now, yet we still could not start the May games without her.

I kept my eyes on the garden entrance and finally saw Jane Kennedy and Maria de Courcelles come in, side by side. But still no sign of the Queen. My eye was caught by a sudden flash of violet and white. There was a tall young man in parti-coloured costume of violet and white coming into the garden, closely followed by a contingent of the guard; and for a wild moment I thought it was George I could see.

That was the very style of George's holiday dress – velvet cap, breeches and doublet of satin, silk stockings – all in those colours of violet and white, with sword-scabbard and shoe-buckles of silver. But this young man was slimmer than George had ever been. And younger, perhaps, since he had no beard...

He came striding straight towards me, laughing, face tilted up to the day's brightness. The sun gleamed off the tendrils of hair escaping from under the violet and white cap; and now I could see they were not the golden-fair of George's hair. They were golden-red. And for each step of that laughing progress, there were ladies curtsying to the ground, men doffing their caps and sinking down on one knee, voices that murmured, "*Your Grace – Your Majesty!*" And I thought I had already known this Queen of mine in all her moods!

I got hurriedly down myself just before she reached me, wondering as I knelt how I had come to forget her love of masquerade. And this, of course, was her favourite one; the one most flattering to her height and her long, slim legs . . . But how had she managed to get hold of George's clothes?

She told me herself, standing in front of me, hands on hips, long legs straddled, the very picture of a deb-onair and handsome young man. "You see me dressed now in these borrowed plumes by courtesy of their owner's brother!' She was laughing again as she spoke, enjoying the impact she was making. "But get up, Will, get up. It is you, and not I, we must all kneel to this day."

I still had my hazel wand in my hand. I turned from her, holding it out to Sir William. He touched me on the shoulder with it, and loudly cried,

"William Douglas, I name you now for this whole day and over all the souls in Lochleven, as – *Lord of Misrule!*"

In the roar of acclaim that followed I rose swiftly and seized the wand of my office from him. I could cut any madcap caper I pleased now. And so at last I had got from Sir William himself the one excuse he would *have* to believe if he observed me in some unusual action. From all that company, too, it was now also my privilege to choose one I could command at any time to follow me and imitate what-ever I myself might do . . .

With my wand raised high and commandingly, I

swung towards the Queen and ordered, "Kneel, then! Kneel, young Sir Parti-colour, and be dubbed, in your turn, my servant."

She went down on both knees before me, arms spread out, head bent, like someone kneeling for execution, her laughing face almost touching the ground. I brought the tip of the wand down on her velvet cap, and cried,

"I name you now, servant to Will Douglas, Lord of Misrule in Lochleven. And for this whole day, I bind you to follow me and obey all my commands."

She scrambled to her feet, calling out for wine to sustain her in the task, and the call was a release that sent everyone surging to the tables. I grabbed my own flask of "wine", rapidly poured a cup for her, then tilted the flask to my lips and drank. Our eyes met as she tasted the contents of her cup. I flourished my flask at her and announced,

"I have drunk a fair amount of this already, young sir, and I intend to drink much more before Lochleven is shut up for the night."

"Then I must also drink more," she answered, "if I am to keep pace with you."

I poured again for her, shouting, "You hear that, my lords, ladies, and gentlemen? You must all drink up, to keep pace with the Lord of Misrule."

They were all only too willing. The wine went round and round till I judged they were merry enough to start the games; and, whooping like a madman then, I led them all off through the garden to get branches of birch for the traditional procession of bringing in Summer. The Queen leaned on my shoulder, pretending breathlessness, as I sent them careering into a thicket of young birch trees. It was our first chance of private talk since my return on

Friday, and we made the most of it.

"*I have got the pearl back from Mr Douglas. Yesterday, by the hand of the Old Lady's maid.*"

"*So you will trust me now for all the details in my note?*"

"*I must. The pearl was agreed on as a sign.*"

"*Then I can promise the two costumes will be in the box, waiting for you.*"

"*And Maria can keep the girls occupied in the inner chamber while Jane and I change!*"

"*Yes — but remember the dangerous point of your exit from the Castle. Sir William sits at supper with the gap at the end of the service screen plainly visible on his left. And you will have to pass over that gap.*"

"*I have my excuse if he sees me. I am following the commands of the Lord of Misrule!*"

She had been quick to understand! I glanced over my shoulder at her, smiling, all ready to tell her of the part Arnault would play at that point of the escape. She forestalled me, her voice suddenly anxious.

"*The pursuit, Will — have you thought of that?*"

"*Of course. We have delayed that as much as we can. You will have a clear start on them.*"

Ellen burst from the bushes crying, "I can hear the musicians. They are coming!"

"Then follow me. Take your branches and follow!" I waved my hand, shouting to her and the others to form up in procession. They came streaming from all directions with their branches of birch held aloft, and fell in behind me as I led their triumphal progress back to the stretch of grass left clear for the dances. The musicians hired from Kinross were already there, banging and blowing away. I shouted to them to change their tune to *The Dance of Robin*

191

Hood, and hastily selected the characters. Arnault, I announced, could be Friar Tuck. He was fat enough. My servant Queen would be Robin. Diderot was big enough to be Little John. Ellen pretty enough to be Maid Marion. Sir William could have the plum role of Sherriff. And I myself would be Point of Arrow, slaying anyone I chose.

Off we went with myself making sure it was the maddest *Robin Hood* ever danced, and with only those "slain" early in the game having any breathing space at all. I kept hold of my flagon, all the same, throughout it all, and made great play of continuing to drink from it. As I did also in *Blind Man's Bluff, The Farmer in the Dell, Poor Roger*, and all the other games that followed.

"There is some devil in you today," the Old Lady told me at last. "I have never seen you quite as mad as this before."

Matters were quieter by then, mostly because I had eventually given them all a chance to sit down and eat. But the Old Lady, I noticed, was only pecking at her food, and she had taken very little of the wine the others were drinking so freely.

"And I always thought you were fond of George," she went on. "But you do not seem to care one bit now that he is going so far from us all."

I leaned towards her, sorry that this part in my masquerade had to be played, but still determined to play it convincingly. "George," I said thickly, "has made only one mistake. He has saddened you by saying good-bye the day *before* my celebration, instead of waiting till the day after it."

The Old Lady pushed me roughly back from herself. "You are heartless! I always said that of you; and now I *know* I was right."

"Not at all, Your Ladyship. Tomorrow I shall care. But today I shall make even you laugh – and that in spite of yourself!"

I was on my feet with the words, and then leaping on to the table. Shouts, yells of laughter, greeted my pose there. I shouted to the musicians to play. They struck up in loud discord, and I went dancing down the length of the tables, teetering from foot to foot among all the cups and dishes littered there, apparently managing to avoid each obstacle only by that miracle of balance accorded to the supremely drunk. Halfway down the tables I struck another pose. The musicians rewarded me with a long drum-roll, and with a flourish of my wand then, I shouted,

"The Lord of Misrule commands! Let Adam now be Eve. Let Eve be Adam!"

We had been merry before, but this was now the signal for licence, and they seized on it as swiftly as they had earlier seized on the wine. Within seconds they had scattered among the shrubbery and were exchanging dress – man with woman, and woman with man. Sir William reappeared wearing the gown that belonged to his child's nurse, and roaring with laughter at himself. The Porches exchanged with their swains. A girl I took to be Muriel ran past me, and turned out to be a kitchen-boy. Diderot came prancing out of the bushes in a dress that met only halfway about his middle, and was followed by a young serving-girl with his doublet billowing amply around her. I myself seized Ellen and traded my holiday clothes for her ethereal blue satin.

I spread the skirts of this in a clumsy curtsy to the Queen, and then led them all off in a wild game of *Follow My Leader*. They came pell-mell after me, all of them exactly imitating me, prancing through the shrubbery, skipping along the top of a terrace wall, dancing around and around the flower-beds, giving tongue the while with the same sounds as I made; crowing like a cock, neighing like a horse... *How long could I keep this up? How long did I need to keep it up? All of them were convinced beyond doubt now that anyone as drunk as I could not have a single serious thought in his head...*

Still wildly dancing I stole a look at the Queen following immediately behind me. Her face had a look of white exhaustion. There were drops of sweat standing out on her skin. It was time to let her rest before the final exertion of the escape. I brought my cavalcade to a halt, and – much to Ellen's disgust – made a further change of clothes with her. If I could divert the company with my own efforts for another hour, I reckoned, that would bring us to five o'clock. The Queen could retire with good grace from the revels then, and her retirement would be the signal for the rest to depart also. With my doublet and sword-belt dangling from one hand, I ran back to the site of our earlier games, all the others following in a ragged tail.

I had always been able to do handstands and other acrobatic tricks. Or since I was seven, at least, I had been able to perform like this. I had been solemnly trying to teach myself to do so one day, all alone on the mainland shore of the loch, when my bumbling efforts had been seen by one of a group of strolling players visiting Kinross. He was an old man, this player, one of the clowns of his group. And he had been scornfully amused at first, by my failures. But then he had started to teach me all his own secrets of balance. And that old man had taught me well!

I threw my doubtlet and belt to Sir William to

hold. He guessed my intention – as indeed he should have done, considering the number of times I had performed for *him*. A shout from him took the place of any announcement I might have needed to make. Some of the guests collapsed to the benches by the tables. The rest formed a wide circle around me. I grinned at them, and called,

"I will perform better drunk than sober, I promise you!"

There was a roar of applause. I judged the space I would have, balanced on the balls of my feet as the old man had taught me, then ran forward to let a double somersault carry me into the last hour of my role as the Queen's jester.

18

I had spent a good part of Saturday cutting and shaping the pegs I meant to drive through the links in the boat-chain. From this, I had gone on to stowing them in my fishing-bag, along with a small iron mallet, and then hiding the bag under the shoreward end of the east landing-stage. There was no-one about there when I went down at the time I had set for myself that evening, and my bag had not been disturbed. Quickly I drew it to me, tipped out the contents, unwrapped the loose end of the boat-chain from the bollard, and set methodically to work.

A peg through every fourth link would be enough to begin with, I had reckoned, and then a peg through every second link. I hammered each one firmly in, rewound the chain on to the bollard, and then stowed my emptied bag and the mallet back into hiding.

I had worked fast, as well as methodically; but I had one more move to make before I was finished. I lifted a pair of oars from one of the boats, and hurried with these to the south-east corner of the courtyard wall. Beside me then, I had the outer aspect of the little round tower where the Queen had first been imprisoned. And there was a window in this outer wall; the one window through which she *could* escape if I failed to get the key to the gate. Always providing, of course, that I could lead her safely across the stretch of courtyard between the main tower and this little one!

The window was fully eight feet from the ground. I upended the oars, leaned them against the wall beneath the window, jammed their blades firmly into the ground, then stood back to give a critical look at my work. With the oars to help her descent, I decided, and with myself waiting underneath to break her fall, she should be able now to get safely down from that window. And if we *were* unlucky enough to be seen crossing the courtyard together, we could still give the excuse that would have served if I had been caught working on the boat-chain. I could protest I was only carrying out another jest in my role as Lord of Misrule. She could plead she was still the servant who was bound to copy all my antics.

I turned and ran back on my tracks, knowing then it would be a matter of seconds only until Sir William finished serving the Queen's supper and came to lock the gate.

The guards there were used to seeing me rush in at the last moment. They let me pass with no more than a glance. Almost immediately on my right then was the retaining wall of the stair leading down from the entrance to the Great Hall. I sidled quickly along its length. The last three steps of the flight projected beyond the south-east angle of the tower. I took a flying leap over the projection; and, safely hidden then from the view of anyone descending the stairs, I ran for the tower's kitchen entrance.

My timing had been exact. I heard Sir William's voice within seconds of gaining concealment in the kitchen doorway. He was talking to Kerr and Newland, both coming off duty as usual at the same time as he went to lock the gate. Sir William sounded as if he had sobered up to the point of being now in a sour sort of mood. Then I heard another voice – Drysdale's. I pressed back into further hiding. He and Sir William were talking about *me*! I caught something from Drysdale about "that boy", and "fooling around with the boats". Had I been seen, after all, from that big east window in the Queen's sitting-room?

The voices of Sir William and Drysdale faded in the direction of the gate. I looked obliquely from my hiding-place and saw Kerr and Newland still standing together, still talking. Were they also discussing some sight of me at the boats? I waited with held breath for the return of Sir William and Drysdale. If there was any delay in dismissing the guards on the gate, I realised, it would almost certainly be because of some suspicion about the boats. I began to pray that Sir William's sour mood meant he would be unwilling to take the trouble of going down to check on these.

Drysdale came back into my view, followed by the guards relieved of duty at the gate. Kerr and Newland turned to greet these two, then the whole group walked on towards the kitchen door. My prayer – if it had been needed – was answered. I moved swiftly into the kitchen, and called out,

"Sir William is ready to be served."

There was a flurry of maids and stewards reaching for the dishes that would be served to the others at table in the Hall. I picked up Sir William's own dish, took a damask napkin from the neatly-folded pile standing ready, then led the procession of servants up the kitchen stairs, past the end of the service screen, and into the Hall.

Sir William was already in his seat at the head of the table, Lady Agnes on his right, the Old Lady on his left, and Lady Lindsay beside the Old Lady. Arnault too, was seated as usual, in the place opposite my own – one that was not too near the family company, yet still not too near, either, to the servants' position below the salt. I placed the dish I carried in front of Sir William, then went to the window immediately to the right of where he sat – the one that gave him a view of Kinross, and that would therefore also let him see any boat heading directly westward from the island. Quietly I began to close the shutters over this west window.

"Leave those!" Sir William bellowed. "What d'ye think you are at, boy – shutting out *my* view without *my* permission!"

"But sir – " I looked innocently around. "It was to protect you. The wind is still from the west. And it has become such a cold one again."

"I fear your page is right, Sir William." Arnault spoke up with a great air of professional gravity. "May is a treacherous month; the time when men – and women too – are subject to chills and rheums of various kinds. And that is the very thing likely to happen to you, if you expose yourself to a cold wind after the exertions *you* have had today."

Sir William eyed him without much favour. "What d'ye mean to imply by that, M'sieu? That I am not entitled to disport myself occasionally, as other men do?"

"Sir William, I am merely saying – " Arnault's

voice flowed smoothly on while I continued my quiet closing of the shutters. Sir William interjected occasional grumbles into the flow, but I could see he was heeding Arnault's advice. Sir William was a fit man, but still always careful of his health! I wondered if I could dare to close the shutters of the north window also, but decided against that risk. The north window would certainly allow Sir William an oblique view of the crossing I had to make; but I still had one card left to play in that part of the game.

The key to the gate was my next objective. It lay where Sir William always placed it when he supped – on the table, close to his right hand. I came back to the table, busily shaking out the folds of my napkin, my eyes fixed on the key's heavy iron shape.

"Your wine, sir?" I leaned towards the flagon of wine in front of Sir William, and grasped it with my right hand. The cup for the wine stood beside the flagon. I let my napkin drop carelessly to the table before I reached for the cup with my left hand. I poured the wine and put the flagon back in place. The napkin had fallen in loose folds that completely covered the key. I put the wine-cup handy to Sir William's grasp, swept up napkin and key together in one servile movement, then bowed myself back from the table.

Arnault had been watching me, and Arnault's tongue became busy again the moment the napkin dropped over the key. "As I was saying, Sir William," he began, "it is not the quantity of wine a man drinks so much as the question of whether he has the stomach for it. Also, I have noted in you, sir, a certain choleric tendency which means you may find an over-indulgence difficult to digest. And if you will pardon me for saying so – "

"Good God, man," Sir William interrupted, "are you daring to suggest I cannot hold my wine?"

The long and hard outline of the key under the napkin was firmly in my grasp by that point. With Arnault launching into a vehement defence against Sir William's charge, I moved unobtrusively from the table and towards the screen. I could count on Arnault to go on with the distraction of his argument. Arnault, I knew, would continue to keep Sir William's attention diverted towards his place on the right of Sir William's own, and therefore away from the sight of the Queen and Kennedy passing the gap at the end of the screen on the left of Sir William's position.

The three-minute time-margin I had counted on was already being eaten into; yet still nothing done in the course of those three minutes could be so hurried as to call attention to myself. I schooled myself to a walking-pace as I left the Hall, went down the outer stair, and around the south-east corner of the tower. Diderot was standing at the entrance to the kitchen, lounging there like a man taking the air after a hard day's work indoors. His cleaver hung from the broad leather belt around his waist, attached there by an inch or so of chain snapped on to a steel ring. He moved forward at the sight of me. I closed with him, and looked up to the south window of the Queen's apartments.

The note I had smuggled in to the Queen had warned her to have Jane Kennedy on watch there. I saw Jane's head peering from the window, and waved upwards. On the instant, Jane withdrew her head. I turned to Diderot and told him,

"Watch out. You will see them in fifteen seconds from now."

Diderot nodded and moved to lean back against the south wall of the tower. I walked soberly away from him towards the gate, counting the seconds as I went. I stood by the gate with the key – still under the napkin – in my right hand, my face turned towards the stair. If I did not see the Queen and Kennedy by the time I had finished counting, *something* would have gone wrong.

The longest fifteen seconds in my life came to an end with the appearance of two figures in red and black at the head of the stairs. They started walking hand in hand down the steps – the tall one and the tiny one, the "soldier's wife" and her "daughter". Some members of the Guard came out of the barracks, noisily arguing with one another as they moved towards the kitchen. The Queen could not see them from her position on the steps. But she had heard them. And she had stopped where she was, on the fourth step from the bottom. One more downward step, she had realised, would bring her into the soldiers' view. And she did not know of Diderot waiting there to protect her passage to the gate! There had been no chance for me to warn her of that precaution.

Someone had to decide what to do. The Queen was motionless still; and Diderot himself would not be able to see her unless she moved the one further step that would also let her be seen by the soldiers. I turned to the gate, unlocked it, then vigorously beckoned to the two figures on the stairs.

The tall one began moving down again, taking the small one with her. Hand in hand at the foot of the stairs, they turned to walk towards the gate. I saw Diderot sauntering into view at their rear, as they walked; but his cleaver still hung at his belt, and there was no outcry from the soldiers still arguing behind the angle of the wall.

I was holding the gate open just far enough to let the two figures pass beyond it. They slipped through the space, with myself crowding on their heels. I closed the gate, relocked it, then got rid of the key by dropping it down the barrel of the cannon beside the gate. My action brought a nervous giggle from Kennedy; but the Queen made no sound. I whispered to her,

"Stay as near as you can to the wall, Your Grace. There may be soldiers on the parapet above us. And keep close behind me."

Rapidly then, I led the way from the gate to the north-eastern corner of the courtyard wall. The east landing-stage lay diagonally ahead from there, and only twenty yards away. I could see my own little boat bobbing at the edge of the shrubbery to one side of the stage. Over my shoulder, I said,

"Walk hand in hand, now, as you did before."

Immediately then I stepped from the sheltering shadow of the wall, and walked quickly to the landing-stage. A swift glance showed me the other two following at the same brisk pace. The landing-stage was clear – no, God damn it! There was someone there – a woman, just rising from the cover of the shrubbery. Minny! It was Minny waiting there. I became aware of the footsteps behind me faltering as she spoke.

"Will . . . I had to come. To say – "

I turned to reassure the Queen just at the moment I realised that Minny – from sheer force of habit, no doubt – was sinking down in a curtsy to her. "No! For God's sake, Minny!" I made a lunge to grasp her and bring her upright again. "You could have us all caught if anyone saw you at that!"

She was trembling, and I had not meant to be so rough. I turned to the Queen and told her. "Get quickly into the boat, Your Grace. And keep well down till I tell you otherwise."

Minny had recovered herself enough to reach for the painter of the boat. I let her continue unwinding it from its bollard while I steadied the boat to let the Queen and Kennedy climb aboard. We came face to face in the moment before I myself leapt aboard; and bravely, Minny finished,

" – to say good-bye, Will."

"Not good-bye – " I bent and kissed her cheek, "– but, 'till we meet again'."

"God keep you, son." I was thrusting with an oar to push the boat out as I caught Minny's last words; but she was out of sight before I had the chance to look up again. I spoke to the Queen and Kennedy, crouching low in the boat.

"I am rowing north just now, to bring us to that end of the island. The trees in the garden will give us cover till we reach it. Once I have cleared the island's north end, I will row north-west to the small island called Alice's Bower. That will keep us just out of sight of the north window in the Great Hall. And Alice's Bower will also give us cover when I turn west there, to head for the New House landing-stage."

I concentrated all my strength of mind and body then, on clearing the north tip of the island and reaching Alice's Bower faster than I had ever done before. There was no movement from the other two, as I rowed. I thought briefly of Minny allowing herself to be locked out for the night so that she could say good-bye to me. Minny would be discovered when the alarm went up. But I *would* send for her. And soon. The Queen spoke softly into my thoughts,

"Sir William saw you tonight at the landing-stage. From my east window."

My stroke grew rough for a moment before I said, "I was holding up the launch of the Castle boats – delaying pursuit, like I said I would."

"I guessed that. I distracted his attention by pretending to faint. And made such a show of it, he was not sure if he *had* seen you, after all."

So it was her quick-wittedness I had to thank for the answer to that prayer I had put up! I steadied my stroke and saw the north tip of the island beginning to drop away from me. A minute later, Alice's Bower loomed up on my left. I oared around for my final change in direction. The island slid past, and we were four minutes from the mainland shore. Gaspingly, I said,

"You may sit up now, Your Grace, and wave your signal to Lord Beaton."

The Queen and Kennedy both struggled up to sit opposite me. The Queen swept the countrywoman's black hat from her head; and I saw that, underneath this, she had bound her hair up in a gauzy veil of red and white. Quickly she unwound this, and with her hair tumbling free then, she rose in the boat to wave the veil back and forwards, back and forwards. Kennedy steadied her as she waved, and it was Kennedy who said,

"There is someone waiting on the landing-stage – an armoured man."

I looked over my shoulder, and immediately stopped rowing. It was not George waiting there. Neither was it Beaton, or Sempil. I hailed the waiting figure loudly, roughly.

"Who are you?"

The answer came back indistinctly, and I thought I caught the name "Wardlaw". But I knew no Wardlaw! I looked up at the Queen and told her,

"This man is a stranger to me."

Quietly she answered, "And to me."

So we could be running into a trap! I opened my mouth to speak the words, but she checked me with one uplifted hand. "Go on rowing, Will," she told me; and calmly seated herself again.

"But, Your Grace – "

"Yes!" she interrupted. "It could be a trap. But what can I do now, except to dare it?" Her eyes flashed suddenly with the light of that first challenge I had seen her give to Lord Lindsay. Straight-backed, with the ring of ultimate authority in her voice, she commanded, *"Go on rowing!"*

I was no longer in charge of the escape. I bent to the oars and pulled the last hundred yards to the landing-stage. The voice of the man there sounded again as I began closing with it.

"Did you not hear me? I am Wardlaw – James Wardlaw, your guide to the rendezvous with Lord Beaton."

I looked back over my shoulder. The man, Wardlaw, had come right to the edge of the stage. He turned, as I looked, and beckoned forcefully in the direction of the boatshed. From beyond the angle of the boatshed wall a band of horsemen came clattering, George Douglas in the lead, Beaton and Sempil riding just behind him.

Wardlaw seized the painter I threw to him, and pulled the boat close to the landing-stage. I leapt ashore, and would have turned then to hand the Queen out of the boat – except that there was no need for me to do so. George had flung himself off his horse and come rushing to the edge of the landing-stage. The others of his band had all followed suit, and there was a score of hands already waiting to help her ashore.

I stood back from the first flurry of greetings, and it was only when they brought the Queen in triumph to the waiting horses that I realised these had only two spare mounts among them. George turned from helping the Queen into the saddle of the first of these spare mounts. His eyes met mine, then went beyond me to where Jane Kennedy stood. I stood watching his indecision and miserably regretting my own failure to warn him she would be part of the escape plan.

The rest of the troop was mounted now, reins gathered, all ready to go. They too were looking towards myself and Kennedy. And so was the Queen. She urged her horse towards us, bent down, and said quietly to Kennedy,

"Jane, my gentle little Jane, I need no-one now to play the lute or to dress my hair for me. But I do need soldiers."

Kennedy smiled up at her. "And I, Your Grace, am glad to be spared the battle that faces you. But I will find myself an outfit, and follow after you, to dress your hair for victory *after* the battle."

Standing on tiptoe, she kissed the face bent down to her. The Queen sat straight again in the saddle, and turned to her escort.

"My lords," she cried. "Gentlemen! I owe my freedom to the boy, Will Douglas. And I will not leave this place till I see him mounted and ready to go with me."

George was already bringing the spare horse up to

me, leading it along with his own. Laughing, he told me, "Mount and ride, Will! Mount and ride!"

I swung myself into the saddle at the same time as he did, laughing along with him. "Beside me, Will!" the Queen cried, and urged her horse towards the waiting figure of Wardlaw the guide.

"Through the village of Lochleven," he called to her, "and then another mile is all you have to the rendezvous."

"*Through the village of Lochleven...*" Did Wardlaw know what he was doing? It was not likely we would encounter opposition in so small a village; but there was no mistaking the identity of the Queen now – not with that mass of red-gold hair tumbled about her shoulders. What would the people of the village do when they saw her; the ordinary people who were neither soldiers nor spies, but simply her subjects? Wht would *their* attitude be to her now?

It was the last but one risk she would have to face before the final risk of the battle with Moray's men, I realised; the risk of being jeered at again, of having such names as Lindsay had used thrown once more in her face. And, I vowed, I would kill any man who dared use these names to her now.

I saw the first of the villagers within seconds of our start – a young man who stared in amazement at first, then smiled, tugged off his hat and bowed low as she passed him. The Queen smiled back, and waved to him. And all through the village it was the same. With each little group of people we passed I saw how right – how gloriously right – Beaton had been in the intelligence sent through George. From each of these little groups I saw that first start of amazement, then smiles, waves, and a bending of the knee to her. And smiling, graciously acknowledging the people's pleasure in her return, the Queen led her troop through them towards the rendezvous.

Once out of the village, however, she called to Wardlaw to quicken the pace; and he did so – with a vengeance, too. A good horse can run a mile in little more than two minutes; and these horses stolen from Sir William were good ones that did not balk at the rough terrain they had to cover before we saw Lord Seton and his troop. They too were riding hard, sweeping down the shoulder of Benarty Hill towards the meeting-point, and there was no slowing in the pace of either troop when they did join us there. Seton simply pointed to the track ahead and shouted,

"Further southwards yet, Your Grace. To Queensferry, and your first resting-place in freedom!"

And then the battle, I thought; the battle that would decide all. The Queen turned a laughing face towards me before she urged her horse to the head of our joint force. And she was so beautiful! The glow of colour on her skin was like the opalescent glow of a seashell. The amber of her eyes gleamed with dark, contrasting brilliance. In the wind of our passage her long hair was like a mass of golden-red light swirling around her head.

She was free; restored to subjects who loved her again, and so she was – she *must* be – riding to victory. And she owed that to *me*. That was the final message I saw then in her beautiful, laughing face; and in the pride and glory of that moment, I could have wept . . .

I did weep, I did weep! With my head leaning on my hands, and the tears slowly dripping on to the courier's report of her execution. I wept for the victory that should have been hers; the victory that was snatched away when the fox, Argyll, failed at the last moment to bring up the support we needed. I wept for her flight from the battlefield, for the mistaken decision to seek a refuge in England, and for all the long years of captivity she had endured there.

Why had she not fled to her own kinfolk in France instead of trusting to the English Queen to help her? Why had she not realised how insecure that woman felt on her own throne – and how much she feared that this beautiful and popular young Scottish Queen would become a focus of rebellion for *her* subjects? I wept for that too; and for the folly of those Englishmen who had finally justified the fears of *their* Queen.

My Mary, My Queen, would have been alive still if the plots of those Englishmen had not given their Queen an excuse to get rid of the "threat" to her throne. *My* Queen had never plotted against the life of that other one. My Queen had only ever wanted them to free her from her English prison. And she had not listened to me. For twenty years I had been master of all the spying and scheming on her behalf; yet still she had not listened when I warned her that those Englishmen's plots were only a trap set to kill her.

I reached a hand blindly to the papers on my desk. Her letter to me lay there, the letter she had written a few hours before her execution. She had made her last will and testament then too. And she had remembered me in that. The wording of the bequest was in her letter – *"to my little orphan, Will Douglas . . ."* I could not bear to read the words again. The letter drifted from my hand.

Now it was Jane Kennedy's letter that lay on top of the other papers; "gentle little Jane" who had got her outfit and gamely followed behind us on that first day's ride to freedom. Jane had been there with her to the last moment of her life. Jane had attended her throughout the whole scene of the execution...

"... I took the scarf that was to bind her eyes and stood in front of her. She bent to kiss me. Her cheek was cold where it touched mine. I was weeping so that I could scarcely see to tie the scarf. She knelt down, spreading her arms wide on either side of her..."

I had seen her kneel like that – in the garden, that May day she had acted the part of my servant. But then she had been laughing as she knelt, laughing with pleasure in the masquerade she was playing, and in anticipation of the freedom soon to follow... My eyes blurred so that I could not read any more.

I dropped Jane's letter also, and sat with my head bowed over it. The door to my study opened and Minny came in, the young courier following behind her. Minny's hair was white now. Minny was old. And my Queen was dead. I heard my own voice reaching out from a daze of anguish,

"All that beautiful hair, Minny. Do you remember that hair? She cut it off so that she could ride as fast as she had to, in her flight from that battlefield. And as far. Sixty miles, Minny. Sixty miles in the saddle on one day with never a complaint out of her, and her wonderful hair cropped as short as my own..."

"Will – " Minny took me by the shoulder and gently shook me. "The courier wants to speak to you."

I looked beyond her to the courier, and Minny moved aside to let him speak directly to me. He was awkward to begin with; his round, innocent face flushing as he told me,

"It was to comfort your distress, sir, that I asked to speak to you. To tell you something about *her*."

I said roughly, "What can *you* tell me? You never knew her as I did."

"Sir, you are wrong! You knew her only as the restless Queen in captivity. I knew her in death. And she was changed then – utterly changed; no longer struggling against her situation, but totally accepting it instead."

The words had burst from him with all the fervour *I* had ever been capable of at his age; and when he saw I did not mean to stop him, he rushed on in a torrent of speech,

"I determined to be there, sir, as soon as I knew that some of the common people would be permitted to view the execution. I saw it all, sir. I saw her enter the hall with none of the pomp or privilege of a Queen allowed to her, but still so calm and dignified that she *looked* royal. And she died firm in her faith, sir. She told her executioners so. She told them also that she trusted in God to receive her spirit. And all this she said with a face so serene that it seemed to us she was almost happy to die."

My Queen, my Mary, my love ... It had taken George Douglas more than eight years of hopeless devotion to her before his longing for children had led him to marry another. But I had never married. The mist in front of my eyes would not let me see the boy, but still I heard him continue,

"And from first to last, sir, she never faltered in anything she had to do. Her speech was clear, her bearing as regal as ever. And her courage, sir – " The boy paused; and then, in a voice that choked with the strength of his feeling, he finished, "The courage of this Queen, sir, was matchless!"

I blinked to clear my sight. The boy was looking beyond me, his eyes filled now with the light of some inward vision. He spoke again, a strangely yearning note in his voice.

"I have heard, sir, how beautiful she was in her young days. But I have still to see a woman more beautiful than she was then. And I swear to you, I do not think I ever shall. Yet it was not her features alone that made me think so. It was something within herself, something – "

Again he paused, groping for words. I heard a ghost whisper in my ear; the sardonic ghost of long-dead, "blindly-devoted" Arnault telling once more his analogy of the honey-pot and the bees. The boy, I thought, did not yet realise what had happened to him. But I knew. I could see how, in the last few moments of her life, the boy had sensed the strange attraction that had never failed to draw men to her. I rose and went towards him, no longer resenting the way he had contradicted when I said *"You never knew her as I did."* Nor could I grudge him this one last memory that was all he had to set against the host of memories that were mine to cherish. I let my hand fall on his shoulder, and told him,

"You will find the words yet, for what you wanted to say."

I felt the quiver that ran through him then. I drew Minny to me with my other hand, while the voice that had so often before cried out in my heart, cried out again, *"My Queen, my Mary, my love . . ."* But I owed that boy something for the way he had given of his own small share of experience in the attempt to comfort me. I owed him, I thought, some acknow-ledgement of *his* feeling. Some right to mourn with me. Quietly I said,

"God will take care of her soul. We can all be sure of that. But we – you and I together, lad – we will remember *her*."

"*Our* Queen!" I sensed the words proudly repeating in the boy's mind as I walked him and Minny from the room with me. And silently again my heart's cry responded, "*My* Mary. *My* love . . ."